About the author

Anne Nelson grew up on a lake in Northern Idaho with aspirations of one day becoming an author. But alas, life tends to take its own direction which may deviate from many a childhood dream. However, with a natural gift for gab, she spent the better part of her adulthood in Alaska, working for several radio stations, in their marketing and sales departments. Copywriting afforded her the chance to show her creative side and open up her imagination, from time to time. Now semi-retired, she lives a quiet life in Nevada, trying her hand once again at writing, something longer than sixty-seconds.

ALL IN A DAYDREAM

Arlene,

Enjoy the read!

Anne Nelson

ALL IN A DAYDREAM

Vanguard Press

VANGUARD PAPERBACK

A CIP catalogue record for this title is
available from the British Library.

ISBN 9781784657642

*Vanguard Press is an imprint of
Pegasus Elliot MacKenzie Publishers Ltd.*
www.pegasuspublishers.com

First Published in 2020

**Vanguard Press
Sheraton House CastlePark
Cambridge England**

Printed & Bound in Great Britain

Dedication

To anyone and everyone who was ever told they couldn't do it.

Yes, you can!

Acknowledgements

Special thanks to EL James; Robert Harling and Roald Dahl for their wonderful creative minds.

PREFACE

The sun felt warm on her face as she relaxed on deck and relished in her sheer bliss.

You need to understand, she never thought in a million years that anyone would choose her as a lover. Past life giving her an inkling.

This was no one-night stand or brief affair either.

Their passion for each other was far beyond physical.

It was like they completed each other. Their stubbornness and flair for a bit of dramatics matched nicely as well.

Even his temper was a bit of a turn-on... except when it wasn't.

But still in the back of her mind she always had this small inkling of doubt; how, out of all the beautiful ladies whom he must have met, women who were younger, slimmer and much prettier... what made him choose her? But he did!

Her heart swells.

Now let's make one thing perfectly clear, he's a hotty with a capital 'H'. I'm talking the whole package including a package that would make any woman say, DAMN! And Thank YOU! The creator or evolution, whichever is your bailiwick, was very kind to this man; in height, a very pleasant six foot one inches, muscular but not over-the-top ripped. More of a three-pack instead of a six-pack in his two hundred and twenty-pound frame. And, oh my, what a glorious backside. This man has it all whether he was coming or going. He has strong facial features, a well-trimmed goatee and gorgeous green eyes... his bald head makes him look fierce and stoic and sexy as hell. One would and could say he is very handsome indeed.

And with all that, he had a kindness about him. A gentleness that surprised her. He wasn't full of himself or carried himself like he was God's gift to women, which he really is and could have easily been totally conceited about it. But wasn't. He was caring, thoughtful, attentive and very loving. And with all his qualities inside and out, he swept her off her feet, and it was truly the last thing she ever expected.

She seriously missed the clues he was giving.

She had a mirror after all and knew she was cute-ish but was well aware that she carried more than her share of excess poundage, and was nine years his senior. And with what she considered too many strikes against her, he still came back again and again. Initially, for coffee one early morning...

That was actually how they met.

A SUNNY TUESDAY

She was enjoying a quiet morning with her coffee, looking out over the lake that gave her such solace. A lone eagle was out looking for some breakfast and the sun was just starting to warm the day.

She was remembering the poem she wrote so many moons ago about her love of the land and lake and the peace they had always brought her.

That morning's peace was interrupted by some idiot making a racket on a jet ski way too early for her liking.

So many of the neighboring cabins had them but they usually didn't break the tranquility of their surroundings quite this early in the day.

When she looked up from her thoughts, she noticed he was much closer than she realized and was speeding by, just one hundred feet off her dock... her first impression of this man was his stellar good looks. She couldn't help but stare at such a handsome face, which she noticed was grinning from ear to ear...he was having a thrilling time on his morning ride and it made her shake her head and smile to herself. To be that carefree... must be nice.

'Stop staring,' she scolded herself.

But then she realized that he was turning back and coming right for her dock. She wondered what he could possibly want.

She sat admiring the view until reality set in. She wasn't dressed for company, still in her favorite sleeping attire; oversized shorts and tank top and of course no bra. Plus, she was wearing an ugly flannel jacket with her name written over the left breast pocket in black sharpie.

A family thing, everyone had one. Her mom made sure every summer that each of them had a new one and the tradition continued to this day.

She couldn't remember if she'd even brushed her hair. Hell!

As he pulled along the side of the dock, she realized he was even better looking than she first thought. Damn. Then he smiled and casually asked, "Good morning, Rebecca, could you spare a cup of coffee? It's a bit chillier on the water than I thought this morning."

Oh my! That smile, that face... how could she refuse? But how did he know her name? Right, it's written on her shirt. 'Idiot.'

With a timid smile and a nod, she headed up the dock with a, "It's Becca and of course. I'll be right back."

Thank goodness. Now she would at least have a chance to look at her hair; the rest is hopeless at this point in time.

Not the first impression she would have hoped for when meeting a very attractive man but then again, passing ships as it were.

More than likely she would never see him again.

Still, she was relieved that she had run a brush through her hair, small favors.

She opened the screen on the upper deck to ask how he took his coffee, went back inside and fixed his, refilled hers and headed back down the stairs to the beautiful stranger now sitting and looking right at her as she made her way to the dock.

Of course, all she could think about… 'don't trip'.

Trust me, it was the right thing to be thinking about.

She had fallen down the stairs once when she was a kid and broken her nose. That summer sucked.

As it turned out his name was Cain Curtis. He was forty-three, a financial advisor and did most of his work via email, video chat and phone calls. He never liked offices much, so after ten years and a decent client base he was able to work remotely so he could enjoy the freedom to travel and of course he got to play more. The perks of planning.

He was easy to talk to or in this case listen to… he told her the basic info and then came alive talking about his new yacht that was moored one cove over. This was his first time on the lake and he loved it. He was planning on trying his luck fishing later that day and asked her if she knew any good spots.

She didn't. Truth was she found fishing a tad boring but loved going out on the water, usually with a good book.

His yacht, named 'SIRA', was on a shakedown cruise for a week to ten days before they planned on putting her in the ocean to set sail for six weeks exploring the waters of Alaska.

And if you're wondering, 'SIRA' is an anagram for 'Simple IRA.' The warped minds of financial advisors. He'd saved twenty years and even helped design her. Proud father or creator… he loved his boat.

She caught herself smiling the whole time he was talking. 'Two ships, Becs, get a grip.'

He also told her how much he liked her A-frame cabin with the add-ons. It looked rustic and fit quite lovely with the surroundings woods as its backdrop.

She couldn't have agreed more. She also liked that he did the majority of the talking.

His life was fascinating to her and so much more interesting than hers.

Which she didn't like to talk about much these days anyway.

So, the only information he really got from her was her name, Rebecca Lynne Jackson. And that she preferred Becca.

After he finished his coffee, he handed her his cup and thanked her again for her kindness to a complete stranger.

She felt a pang of sadness in that remark.

As he stepped down on the jet ski he looked up and asked, "So, Becca, if it's okay with you, I would like to come back tomorrow for another cup."

"Sure," she replied way too quickly.

She again admonished herself. 'Stop acting like a smitten schoolgirl.'

As he donned his lifejacket, he looked back at her and prompted, "Good, because tomorrow you get to do all the talking."

With a wave and a wink, he fired up the jet ski and took off like a bat out of hell.

She caught herself grinning and that small wink made her feel flushed.

As he was getting farther away, she began to feel a bit lonely. She admonished herself for the third time in less than half an hour… 'get a grip you idiot.' And with that, went about getting her day started.

These days she wasn't doing anything very exciting. She found by keeping things simple and routine… she didn't get as depressed and it helped if she kept a bit more active as well. So, one day pretty much looked like the day prior and even the day before that.

She'd go for a late morning or early afternoon swim every day. The lake was cool but the sun always warmed her quick enough.

She tended to burn so no more than a half an hour in the sun after her stimulating dip.

That way she got a healthy glow as opposed to looking like a boiled lobster.

Too many times as a kid she remembered the pain of a sunburn. A few times as a stupid teenager too. Back in her early years, her parents had a hell of a time getting her out of the water. The cold water wasn't an issue back then. It was her favorite part of summer. Favorite part of her entire year.

Too soon would the leaves turn and school would start followed by a cold winter. But summer would return and she and her lake would be reunited again. Happiest time of her life.

During this quiet time at the cabin, she would always make time to read a chapter or two or even ten some days; the latter was usually on rainy days that messed up her schedule.

She would text or email her best friend and some days even called and chatted. Mary didn't like her alone all the time so that was their agreement. If she wasn't careful, four or five days would go by and she'd get a lecture from Mary about keeping the lines of communication open. It's what best friends do after all.

She would eat her apple, have a protein shake and sometime in the course of the day she might eat some cottage cheese or a KIND bar.

She would also clean up around the cabin every day which included making her bed.

She always thought that was the dumbest thing since she was all by herself and who the hell would care.

But none the less, she would tidy up all the same. Bed included. Again… routine.

18

She also enjoyed walking in the woods above the cabin, trying to calm her mind and to just enjoy the quiet solitude it provided her.

This day's walk after her dip in the lake was a bit different... this day someone else was invading her subconscious.

Basically, she couldn't stop thinking about the next morning's coffee date with the ever-so-stunning Mr Curtis.

She spent most of that day's stroll wondering if she could create a more interesting life between now and then.

That made her laugh at herself. Thank goodness no one was around to witness her outburst.

No great epiphany was forthcoming, so she gave up.

Best to just be truthful... mostly. Some baggage needed to be stored and locked away... forever.

The one thing she decided that would be happening before his arrival, she would be showered and dressed this time around. And she'd definitely need to have on a bra. And not be wearing that unflattering but comfy flannel shirt. It's the little things that made her smile these days.

Back from her walk– some would call a hike –she stared into the refrigerator with the hopes of inspiration. She was a bit hungry since she had walked a bit farther than normal but didn't really feel like fixing anything. A protein shake would suffice for her late afternoon's sustenance. Little fact, she didn't like food much these past few months.

This time of the day she enjoyed sitting in the living room with its wall of windows shaped like a triangle (A-frame) and watching the sun make its arch over the lake. Sunsets on the lake were magnificent.

Too soon it would be pitch black over the lapping water with just a few twinkling lights from other cabins in the distance and of course the millions of stars above.

Her mind always wandered this time of night. This evening she was trying to decide when she needed to run to town for a few supplies, including drinkable water. Maybe she should do a load of laundry or two while she was there. Maybe tomorrow after coffee or the day after that. She didn't really like town. Small but hectic.

That was the nice thing about the cabin... no need to be in a hurry... it promoted procrastination.

Darkness had arrived just after nine p.m. She switched on the light next to the couch and settled in for the evening.

Maybe a movie tonight.

A TRYING WEDNESDAY

She didn't sleep well these past several months and last night was no exception.

The leg cramps weren't as bad as they used to be and she attributed that to all the swimming and hiking she'd been doing. Her legs were getting some great muscle tone and that thought made her smile.

But still she tossed and turned, restless. And still very tired.

She was hoping that coming back to her childhood cabin, away from everything else going on in her life would help. And it did, but not when the darkness came. And she wasn't always referring to the night.

But some evenings it was like a switch... as soon as she tried to sleep her mind seemed to wind itself up and the respite her body wished for and desired was denied by the thoughts that continued to haunt her.

Grief is a process and although she could rationalize it for the most part... sometimes the darkness would overtake her mind.

And on occasion her heart got its own way and sadness and despair would almost suffocate her.

This night her thoughts were a combination of sadness and wants. The wants were more sexual in nature. She was human after all.

But she did wish she was a bit thinner, a bit prettier and a bit more sensuous.

If wishing made it so.

'Come on, Becs, get a clue, buy a vowel. Fantasies are for the young.' Admonishing herself sometimes helped.

This left her feeling guilty and sad for feeling anything at all.

Are those hopes and desires even allowed to a widow? Well shit!

Six a.m.– Really!

The knock on the door put her heart in her throat as her eyes flew open. Who the hell could be here at this time of the morning?

She hadn't slept well, her head hurt and truth be told, it's just too damn early. Not a morning person some days.

She was in half a mind to turn over and try to get another hour of zees, but a second wrap on the door jarred her out of bed.

Half asleep she opened her bedroom door and glanced out to see Mr Jet Ski, aka Cain Curtis, waiting in all his glory on the other side of the front door.

She did her best to catch her breath. Damn, that man was handsome.

So much for looking better... CRAP!

Why did he have to look so fabulous at this hour of the day?

So not fair.

With a shake of her head and a yawn she went and let him in. Not bothering to grab her flannel shirt. Or smile for that matter.

He was smiling enough for the both of them.

'She must look a fright.'

The cabin was chilly and the coffee wasn't made.

While she set to remedy the coffee situation, she asked if he would start a fire.

The cabin did have electric heat but a nice fire was always a much better way to heat the small space.

He was making good work getting the fire going, coffee was brewing and while he was busy, she excused herself to the bathroom.

The mirror said it all; she looked tired and the darkness under her eyes was getting more noticeable... at least to her.

Well at least she could wash her face and run a brush through her bed head before she needed to wake up her inner hostess.

Time to go be courteous to her very early morning guest.

DAMN that smile.

He informed her, "Coffee's ready, I helped myself. Thought we'd sit in the living room since it's so nice and warm with the fire going." And patted the seat next to him on the couch.

With a nod she went to get herself a cup in the hopes the caffeine would wake up her brain. After all, she was supposed to carry the conversation this time around.

As she headed out of the kitchen, she grabbed her flannel shirt and wrapped herself up... she was in her usual sleep attire; shorts and a T-shirt but the no bra thing made her feel self-conscious. And even though she didn't need the extra layer now that the blazing fire had warmed up the living room very nicely, she felt less exposed in the ugly shirt.

As she sat down next to this way too beautiful man, she glanced up through the bay windows and realized that his yacht was sitting about one thousand feet out in the lake. It was huge, had to be one hundred feet or more, and beyond anything she'd seen on this lake, plus it took up every bit of her windows even at that distance.

Without thinking and mostly talking to herself she conveyed in a very serious tone, "That is one huge ass yacht... doesn't really fit on this lake. It's like a pimple on a supermodel. You just don't expect to see something like that here."

Her gaze was broken by a coughing sound and she looked over to see her guest with coffee all over his lap.

She missed him spraying himself with the hot beverage, apparently after her unexpected remark.

The sight made her laugh and then she got the giggles... his expression was priceless and she had to put her coffee down so she didn't spill it over herself.

He didn't seem at all amused and headed into the bathroom. That made her laugh even harder; so hard in fact she was crying and trying to catch her breath. She thought she might be on the verge of hyperventilating.

While he was still cleaning up, she did her best to compose herself.

She hadn't laughed like that in a very long time and it felt strange and good at the same time.

When he came out, he smirked at her and she managed a weak 'sorry', to which he replied, 'no you're not' and she confessed, 'not really, no'.

That dazzling smile returned to his face and she knew all was forgiven.

That definitely was a mood lightener and one hell of an icebreaker. Cain reclaimed his seat next to her on the couch, this time taking her hand in his. A bit unexpected but nice. His hand was warm and she liked seeing hers intertwined with his.

She felt a surge of electricity all the way to the pit of her stomach and below... she was sure she was blushing but he gave no indication that he noticed.

She finally had to ask him why he wasn't off with some leggy blonde. One suited to his amazing good looks.

His look was humorous and something else. And with a squeeze of her hand he smiled, "I am."

Blush deepened and her heart swelled a bit too. 'What a sweet man, even for a liar.' She just grinned.

Then he got back to the task at hand. "Now you don't get to ask any more questions and we've concluded the comedy side of this morning's coffee. I believe it's your turn to talk. Tell me all about yourself."

There it was, the question she didn't want to answer.

She would rather talk more about his yacht and his upcoming trip to Alaska but his gaze made her realize he wasn't talking, he was waiting... waiting for her to tell her tale. 'Fuck.'

She wasn't sure where to start or how much he needed or wanted to know so she took a different tactic and started talking about the cabin, which he said he liked, and about growing up on the lake.

Safe enough and better than anything going on in her current life.

"My brother and I inherited the cabin about four years ago after we lost our parents. Just a few months apart actually. One cancer and the other a broken heart in the guise of a heart attack. Anyway, we share it and the expense now and we divvy up the sixteen-week season which includes his kids. I don't have any, so it works out pretty well, and he gives me first dibs on any weeks or even a whole month if I wish. The cabin has been in our family for over sixty-plus years. My dad and grandfather built the original A-frame back in the '50s. The kitchen and bedrooms were added as the family grew. My brother and his two sons handle most of the upkeep, which is huge. We don't want to sell if we don't have to. It has all my childhood memories." She hoped he would be happy with her tale and not press for more current information.

As she took another sip of coffee, she realized she'd forgotten to test her numbers… CRAP!

She never forgets.

She withdrew her hand from his as she stood which made him stand as well.

"I'm sorry, I just need to test my blood really quick. Help yourself to another cup of coffee if you wish," and made her way into the bedroom, shutting the door behind her.

She was so mad at herself!

Admonishing herself, 'Fuck! Becs, you idiot… you never forget to check. It's not like you're new at this shit… even if you were distracted by an overly handsome man who arrived a tad earlier than expected.'

She put a drop of blood on the strip and waited the few seconds for the monitor to beep, which told her that her numbers were still low… too low… like they've been the past few months. Ever since she gave up eating for the most part but she still liked to check them every day. Mainly to alert herself to the fact that some mornings, she needed to force herself to eat something right away. This wasn't one of them, thank goodness.

She wrote down the number in her ledger. Routine.

This was a personal issue and one that she didn't feel an explanation was required to someone she'd just met. If asked she'd just keep it vague. Not anyone else's business anyway.

She knew that she would need to eat soon but knew it could wait until after he leaves. She'd like to avoid another one of the headaches that have been plaguing her these past few months. Pretty much daily if you must know.

She exited the bedroom with her apologies for the interruption. And retook her seat next to him on the couch.

He had a fresh cup of coffee and looked at her with concern and curiosity.

"What were your numbers? I assume you're diabetic? For how long?"

She sat back after retrieving her coffee and taking a breath before her next drink.

She looked up into his caring green eyes and responded... "I'm sorry but no one asks me that; well, not in a very long time anyway. But my numbers are fine and I've been diabetic just over two decades now. Too long to forget to check them. Anyway, I appreciate your concern but I'm good. Really."

She hoped that would end the disease portion of this morning's conversation.

He retook possession of her hand and squeezed it gently saying, "Please don't be coy and I hate vague. So, how about you tell me what your fasting numbers were, exactly?"

Well that laid one of her questions to rest... he apparently did know something about diabetes.

But then she wondered why he cared.

They didn't really know each other and still she knew somehow that he wasn't going to drop this line of questioning.

With a slight sigh she gave in and told him that she tested with a sixty-four.

His face acknowledged this and he thanked her for her honesty.

Now she wondered how much he knew about fasting numbers. He did know what they were called… which the average person usually doesn't.

She didn't have to wonder very long.

Dropping her hand and standing like some sort of action was required, he stated matter-of-factly. "That's too low. What did you have for dinner last night? I think you need to eat breakfast. But I noticed while getting milk for my coffee that your refrigerator doesn't contain very much food. Perhaps you should just come out to the yacht with me for a good meal."

He was still standing like he meant to take her there now?

'What?'

'Before a shower?'

Too much reality and all before she finished her first cup of coffee.

Anyway, that was a lot to take in from someone she's only just met.

She didn't like it when people got a bit overbearing in regards to her eating habits. Truth be told she didn't like to talk about food with anyone except maybe her best friend, who understands her situation more than most these days.

Her journalism teacher would say that she buried the lead earlier when she was talking about herself. Or avoiding talking about herself. 'Oh, shut the fuck up.'

She hadn't really told him anything personal, yet.

And she didn't want to now, but he was standing there like a statue.

'A Greek god no less, 'wandering thought. 'FOCUS.'

Her expression showed she was feeling a bit deflated. She just wanted to have a cup of coffee and stare at the pretty man. Now look how things turned out.

'Rein it back in, Becs… no time like the present to tell him the whole truth.'

She patted the seat beside her, like he did earlier, in the hopes he'd sit and listen to her confession of sorts.

He slowly acquiesced but didn't take her hand this time. He leaned back, crossing his arms and giving her an 'I'm waiting' look.

It reminded her of someone… but who?

She took a huge breath and began. "For me that really isn't that low. I've had so much worse. Fact is I don't eat meals per se and it's not like I can't afford to miss a few (patting her midriff) but let's be clear, I do eat. I'm not starving myself, really."

He shifted like he was about to interrupt her and she held her hand up letting him know she wasn't finished, and continued.

She could tell he was getting a tad miffed but wasn't exactly sure why. 'Lighten the fuck up.'

"Just about six months ago my husband of over twenty years died. He was having health issues for quite some time and even though it came as a bit of a shock it wasn't totally unexpected. It wouldn't be called a happy marriage but grief is grief. So, for the month following his death, I didn't eat much and when I did, I just threw it back up so I started to avoid eating. During that same timeframe I managed to reverse my days and nights... I would sleep better during the light hours and when the sun would set, I spent my nights swimming, reading and taking long walks. I relished the darkness and on occasion I would be forced to eat. Mostly when the headaches were unbearable or when I'd wake with night sweats, well day sweats really: anyway, that was and still is a tell that my numbers are crashing. And the only time being alone is still very scary for me. But, I found that protein drinks always seem to stay down and that saved me. At night, I found my peace and I was able to avoid people... the sad looks, the 'I'm so sorry for your loss crap' and the interference in my life that I just didn't want at the time."

She raised an eyebrow at him to let him know he was also crossing a bit of a line.

But finished her way too long explanation. "For whatever reason that helped with a lot of the grief. Still working on survivor's guilt. Slowly I've been able to add actual food back into the mix. My best friend finally got

31

me to come around during the daytime hours and helped me turn my days and nights back around. Sleeping at night however, is still an issue sometimes, but I'm trying. As for eating… meals. I still can't handle that very well. But like I said, I do eat, just not the way most do. I have always had an issue with excess weight and this helps me control something in my life which has been a tad out of control these past few months. And in saying all that, I do appreciate your concern." She felt totally drained, mentally, after that very personal soliloquy.

She hadn't told that story to very many people.

She picked up her coffee and finished the last swallow before looking over to see his expression.

Suddenly he was up again but this time he reached over and pulled her into a huge bear hug. It felt so amazing. She wrapped her arms tightly around him hoping he wouldn't let go. She hadn't had a hug like that in what seemed like forever. And whether he sensed that or felt the same, he didn't let her go for several minutes. She felt warm and safe in his arms. And to her surprise, it felt like she belonged there.

When the embrace did end his look wasn't one of anger or even one of pity but there was something in his look that made her wonder if this would be the last morning, they would ever have coffee together. The last morning, she would ever see him again.

'Who could blame him, Becs? You got baggage, girl.'

Still, she knew she would miss him.

Again, it's like he could sense what she was thinking.

"I won't bug you today about eating. Although I think you should and soon. I do want to thank you for confiding in me. It means more than you realize. I am sorry for your loss and maybe one day we can have a longer conversation about that. But for now, I think you need rest and as I stated before, food. And just an FYI… tomorrow morning's coffee better be served with bacon, eggs and toast or you and I are going to have a problem, okay?"

The stern look he was expressing was actually very sexy but all she could think about was 'he's coming back tomorrow'. This gave her heart an extra beat or two and with an affirmative nod he gave her a peck on her cheek and took his leave.

She was sure she was blushing again but she didn't care. He kissed her cheek and was coming back. Two things that made her whole day.

Holy shit, that's who he was reminding her of; Christian Grey of Fifty Shades. She had just read all five books a few months back. Lots of hours during the night. Giving her loads of time on her hands to read.

The sound of the jet ski made her jump. Bringing her out of her thoughts

She couldn't help but laugh at herself, again.

Breakfast consisted of an apple and a small spoon of peanut butter. And meds of course.

'Fuck, I need to run into town for groceries.'

It was still early enough to get everything done in town in one trip so she headed to the bathroom for a shower.

The warm water always felt good to her but she hated the small little box they called the shower.

It was made for an RV but her dad felt it fit the space... very little space as it turned out.

Her nephew asked if he could remodel the bathroom but money was tight that year so they promised to revisit the issue the following summer.

He was her brother's oldest kid and had three little ones of his own. Another generation growing up at the cabin. His little brother was single and loving it.

She missed her dad and mom. Like she told Cain, it had been four years now since they passed away but the cabin was filled with so many memories of them. In some ways it was like they were still there. And that gave her a comforting thought.

Dressed and looking a tad more put together than before... she sat at the kitchen table to make a to-do list for town.

It's always helpful since it was a forty-minute drive, one-way, and going back for a missed item wasn't a practical option.

Fill the seven empty water jugs.

Bathing and washing dishes in lake water is acceptable but for all else you need drinkable water. Rustic isn't always fun.

Towels, sheets and dirty clothes to the Laundromat.

Both of those tasks can get done at one place which is always helpful.

Groceries

> Apples
> Cottage Cheese
> Orange Juice
> Eggs
> Bacon (center cut a must)
> Jam
> Bread
> Coffee Creamer (sugar free)
> Milk
> Protein Shakes
> Glucosamine snack bars (perfect for a quick snack and to help keep her sugars level throughout the day.)
> Hot Sauce
> Butter

Living alone you tend to talk to yourself and she was no different.

"Wow, I really don't have much in the refrigerator right now. Well, that should be enough. It's just breakfast after all."

Water jugs and laundry loaded in the back of her SUV. Purse, keys and cell phone in hand. Eight-thirty a.m. — time to head to town.

She glanced down at the lake from the top of the hill where she parked and realized the yacht was still there. From this vantage point she could see a good portion of the lake and still the gigantic boat was out of place but lovely all the same. She wondered if he was going to stay there all day. She couldn't make out people on the yacht so she knew this far in the tree line, she was invisible to the naked eye.

She always thought she'd like the ability to be invisible when she chose. Weird thought. She shook her head at herself.

'Daylight's burning. Time to get my ass in gear' and with that thought she climbed in, started her Enclave and drove towards the main road that would lead her to her final destination.

For a small town it had its share of traffic, which meant bad drivers and she never had patience for stupid people who didn't know how to use a turn signal.

First stop was the Laundromat and she was pleased that it wasn't busy, for once. Laundry started and water jugs filled, she just needed to sit and wait to put everything in the dryer.

Crap, she forgot her book. And the magazine selection was weak.

But across the road and down a block was a coffee shop. That should kill a bit of time and another cup won't hurt since she was getting sleepy sitting in the warm and humid environment.

Fully caffeinated and laundry done… it was time to head to the grocery store. Joy.

List in hand, she grabbed four reusable bags from the back of her SUV and got a move on to finish the task at hand.

She added iced tea to the cart along with a pre-packaged salad mix but other than that, kept to the list.

Her stomach growled while waiting to check out, a tad embarrassing but no one seem to take notice.

She went ahead and grabbed a KIND bar and added it to her stack. That should curb the hunger and it's easy to eat while she drove back to the cabin.

She couldn't wait to get out of town.

Back to where she began just after one.

And the yacht was gone.

That left her with a twinge of sadness.

She parked at the top of the hill, debating for two seconds whether or not to drive down to the lower lot… truth be told she was scared of the hill. It was a steep decline so she avoided driving down it whenever possible.

She did have a cart to put everything on but if she put too much weight on it, it would reach the bottom way before she did.

Yes, found that out the hard way.

'Fuck it. Two trips won't kill me.' Good pep talk to herself.

Gingerly she rolled the water jugs and laundry to the bottom, unloaded and headed back up to get the groceries.

Finally, back in the cabin she began putting everything away.

Quite happy that the fridge looked nice and full. Small cabin refrigerator, really didn't take a lot.

In the last bag she found her KIND bar, oops.

'Maybe later.'

She was sweaty and stressed from town and couldn't wait to take a swim; it's her favorite activity of the day.

The water was glorious and she started to do her version of laps before the chill of the lake got to be too much.

She climbed out and laid on the dock to let the sun warm her body back up.

She decided to stay out a bit longer than normal, enjoying the heat of the day.

Back in the cabin she grabbed a water, the KIND bar and her book and made herself comfy on the couch.

She had several hours until sunset so might as well get her read on.

Great idea in theory.

But the warmth of the day and lack of sleep the previous night put her right out for a well-needed nap.

She woke groggy and feeling too warm, just as the sun was making its early evening arch on its way to nightfall.

She sat up, discarded the blanket and finished the water in one huge gulp followed by the last half of her KIND bar.

Afternoon naps always messed with her sleeping at night.

Plus, now she was stiff and the headache was back.

She knew what would help.

An evening swim would cool her down and take away the stiffness from her impromptu slumber.

The sun was nice enough to dry her suit... no skinny dipping for her... too old and way too embarrassing, even on moonless nights.

She loved swimming at this time of the evening. It was comforting, the cool waters all-encompassing her.

Ten minutes later, she felt refreshed and even her head gave up its ache... 'thank you very much.'

As she climbed the ladder on to the dock, she realized that the yacht wasn't back.

Probably safely moored in one of the many bays around the lake.

She wished him a silent, 'sleep well and I'll see you for breakfast.'

Now in pajamas she thought she should have a light supper... another protein shake will suffice. And with drink in hand settled in to watch some mindless drivel on TV.

Her brother can't live without his sports and installed a satellite dish a few years back. And it did come in handy on occasion.

She usually didn't care about watching television but tonight channel surfing was mildly entertaining.

As she was getting ready for bed, she decided to set her alarm clock. A precaution mostly; she wanted a failsafe making sure she was up early enough to get everything prepped for her breakfast with the ever-alluring Cain Curtis. Well that and she'd really like to have clothes on.

Novel idea.

She didn't so much like the sound of eating as much as she did cooking for someone, and cooking for him made it all the better.

Full on dark. Lights out!

A FRUSTRATING AND MAGICAL
THURSDAY

She woke startled... not because of the alarm sounding but she was drenched with night sweats and her hands were shaking.

"FUCK ME!" She tried to remember everything she'd eaten yesterday... 'moot point now, you idiot.'

She got up and grabbed her testing kit. As she sat at the kitchen table, she turned on the overhead light and dimmed it to a nicer and less in-your-face brightness and proceeded to test her blood... holy shit thirty-four, way beyond low. Dangerously low in fact. She was feeling nauseous and her head was pounding.

Like she told her new acquaintance, this is the only time she hated living alone. She knew what to do to remedy the situation but it still scared her a bit.

She got up and poured a small glass of the orange juice... thinking of a scene from 'Steel Magnolias'... "juice is better".

Wow, the mind is an odd piece of work.

She couldn't help but shake her head at herself and downed the OJ in two swallows. She knew that wouldn't be enough for such low numbers so she went back in the bedroom where the small pantry was and fetched the peanut butter. She knew it was a good way to get her numbers up.

She didn't want to eat too much... it's still all fat after all, but she managed to consume a large teaspoon of peanut butter, which by the way, tastes like crap when eaten after drinking orange juice.

Head in hands... she laid them on the table. She felt exhausted.

Now to wait, ten minutes at least to give her body the chance to claim what she ate. Then she'd check her numbers again.

Second go-round was fifty... better but not great and it also meant that going back to sleep wasn't the best of ideas.

The clock read three forty-five a.m.

Probably because of her long nap, she didn't feel all that tired and her guest is apparently an early riser so she opted to stay up.

At least she'll get in that shower and be dressed before his arrival. About the only positive in this morning thus far.

While the hot water took the chill out of her clammy skin, her mind veered and she hoped he wouldn't ask what her numbers were... she didn't want to have that discussion again today. And even though they didn't know each other well... he seemed to really care. But it's so personal so she made the decision to avoid any major battle; she would just lie.

Small favor, in that the big-ass boat wasn't out front to see her lights on this early in the morning.

Okay, hair and body all washed, time for clothes.

Yep, even a bra.

That made her smile to herself.

This morning she actually used the blow dryer on her wet head since the cabin was really quite chilly.

This would be the most put together she's ever looked for their morning coffee... despite the rough beginning to her day.

'Now let's get the chill out of the cabin.'

She wasn't the best fire builder but she managed to get it going, "Well, shit!"

She burned her palm.

This day was really starting to piss her off.

She ran her hand under the cold water and noticed it was quite pink... 'fuck.'

At least no blisters, yet.

She dug out the Neosporin and put a good amount on the burn before covering it with a rather large Band-Aid.

Sarcastically and aloud, "That's not noticeable. Well this should be a great conversation starter."

And with that, lights went on full power in the kitchen as she went to get the coffee ready.

She also washed the glass and spoon she used earlier before setting the table for two.

Everything she touched made her palm hurt but she did manage to keep it dry when washing the two items.

Damn, it was still way early... too early to put the bacon in the oven and she didn't want to start the coffee quite yet, even though she so wanted a cup.

She settled for a yogurt. Her head was starting to ache again and she knew her numbers were still too low.

'This day sucks out loud.'

She didn't bother to turn the lights on in the living room since the fire gave her just enough ambient light. And the kitchen light was more than adequate. She sat on the couch eating her yogurt watching the fire.

She loved the fire; it reminded her of happier times with her family and growing up on the lake. Her dad was always the first one up and had the cabin nice and warm before anyone was even awake. Those memories always made her smile.

Okay, yogurt finished, headache a dull annoyance, palm throbbing but finally there's a hint of the sun in the sky... it's now four thirty a.m.

No more waiting; she needed coffee and headed back into the kitchen.

The face in the door window, although stunning, scared the living crap out of her. She jumped, dropping the spoon and yogurt container on the floor. She's pretty sure she said 'Fuck' out loud as well.

How in the hell did she not hear that loud ass jet ski?

Before she opened the door, she picked up her items, depositing the spoon in the sink and the container in the trash and hit the brew button on the coffee pot.

44

He at least looked apologetic as she opened the door. He should, she thought.

He pulled her into another bear hug with a, "good morning, beautiful."

Who could stay mad at this man when he was so damn sweet and smelled amazingly good?

He released her and took her damaged hand in his. "How bad? I saw a light come on pretty early. Are you okay? And don't think I didn't notice the yogurt. What were your numbers this morning?"

Well, okay... nothing seems to get by him. Even at O-dark thirty. Suddenly she was feeling tired.

With the sun lighting this early morning sky, she could now see that his yacht was indeed anchored close by. It was to the left of her living room windows, more in front of the dock. Explains a lot. 'Doesn't he sleep?'

Of all the mornings to have this cascade of shit happen, it would be the morning he was coming for breakfast.

'And why does he look so good in jeans, T-shirt and his own flannel shirt? So not fair.'

She countered, "How come I didn't hear the jet ski this morning? Do you not sleep? Or are you spying on me? Worried I wasn't going to feed you?" Thinking maybe humor might work. Nope!

An impasse... they stared at each other for a few moments before he broke the silence. "You first."

"Then I need coffee."

And with that she got out two cups and poured them each some of the lovely brew. She handed him the milk and a spoon as she fixed hers.

She figured they might as well stay in the kitchen and pulled out a chair at the table. She really just wanted to lay her head down at this point.

He was having none of that and took her hand, gingerly, looking at the bandage again and led her to the couch.

Setting down his coffee he reached over and turned on the side lamp to make it a bit lighter. And again, patted the seat beside him telling her where he wanted her to sit.

She took a much-needed fix of caffeine before she shook her head and started to answer his questions.

"It's not blistered, just pink and I have it thoroughly covered in ointment. And yes, before you ask, I suck at building fires. And if memory serves, I mentioned yesterday that sleeping isn't always easy for me and some mornings I just don't fight it. And since I was up too early for coffee, I decided to have a yogurt. Now, it's your turn."

He shook his head. "Nope… you left out a few details. And since you look tired; more than tired, you look exhausted, Becca. And your coloring is off. You look really pale. And it's more than you just couldn't sleep, So, what were your numbers and please don't make me ask again."

She wasn't going to have this conversation. And he seriously had a few traits of 'Fifty shades'.

She felt better now and it's a very intrusive line of questions.

But, how could she tell him that without him getting his hackles up like yesterday?

She realized she must have been a bit slow in answering, lost in her thoughts, when he took her face in his hands. Looking right into her eyes, "I know it's none of my business but I happen to care about you and I want you to always be honest with me, like you were yesterday. So, please stop overthinking and just tell me."

How does he do that? He seems to see right through her.

Shit! 'I could lie. I should lie!' Passing thought.

She took another drink of coffee and with a nod, set to confess yet again, second day in a row in fact.

She really hated this and her tone might have conveyed that a bit too much.

"Fine, I woke up just before four this morning with night sweats and the shakes… my numbers were a very concerning thirty-four if you must know. So, I got up and had some OJ and peanut butter and got them back up. But after my shower I knew I needed to eat something else to keep them from dropping further, hence the yogurt. I tried to take care of it all before your arrival because it's my problem and I didn't want this discussion again and truth be told, I'm not used to having someone worry about me." Then added with a bit too much sarcasm, "How's that working out?"

She couldn't read his expression entirely but when he stood and walked out of the living room, she knew that miffed was an understatement.

She figured he was leaving and waited to hear the front door open and close.

But that didn't happen.

'Huh!'

She could hear him moving around in the bedroom but there was no sound that gave away what he was up to and she didn't want to follow him since she knew he was pretty pissed off and she knew she had caused it.

She also thought maybe she should apologize but then again maybe he shouldn't be so nosy.

She felt so drained again.

Her heart jumped when, out of her silent thoughts, he was right beside her with a resounding and a bit loud, "Start breakfast, now!"

She didn't overthink that statement twice.

She was up and at the fridge in seconds pulling out the center-cut bacon and the eggs she bought the day prior.

It was a small kitchen stove so she laid out six strips of bacon on a baking sheet, turned the oven to three hundred and seventy-five and cracked five eggs in a bowl with half a cup of milk. Two slices of bread in the toaster and she poured him a freshly squeezed glass of orange juice, all without making eye contact.

He was sitting at the table now, and she knew without looking that he was closely watching her every move. And he was still clearly agitated.

She put the glass of juice in front of his placemat and returned back to the task at hand.

She was startled again when he suddenly broke the silence.

Man, he was good at that. 'Damn.'

"As I'm sure you noticed, the yacht is in fact out in front of your cabin again this morning. Mainly because I knew I was coming here first thing. And now I'm doubly glad she's there since I've packed you a bag and you'll be joining me for the duration of my stay on the lake. It appears you need looking after. AND, if you so much as make any attempt to argue I will take you over my knee, which is what I wanted to do after your sarcastic statement earlier. And DON'T think for a minute I won't. I didn't come by jet ski this morning; I brought the launch… its quieter and safer. And again, I'm glad I did since you'll be coming back with me. And for your final two questions… yes, I sleep just fine usually but something told me to keep an eye on you, and I'm glad I did. And no, the thought of you not cooking breakfast hadn't occurred to me."

The oven beeped to indicate it was at the desired temperature, so she placed the bacon in and shut the door and set the timer for fifteen minutes. She then got to work seasoning and whisking the eggs into a frothy mixture.

She was of course biding time, and taking everything, he said and putting it into context before responding. Wow, that was quite the speech.

She actually believed his threat and decided perhaps to just ignore everything until after breakfast. Maybe by then she could reason with him. And wondering if he'd understand his new nickname, 'Fifty'. Twitchy palm and all.

She smiled to herself, making sure he wouldn't see.

A less stressful time might be better before she called him that.

He didn't let the silence last very long. He always seemed to know when she was deep in thought and just when to speak to scare the tar out of her.

"I see you're overthinking things again. You're not going to change my mind and no; I don't think I'm being unreasonable at all or overreacting."

She couldn't help but look right at him with a telling look that made him smile. He was on target with what she was thinking and looking a tad smug about it too.

Yep, 'Fifty' is a very fitting nickname.

Exasperated by this man, she headed to the living room to retrieve her cup and poured herself another coffee.

Forgetting all her hostess duties she didn't even ask if he'd like another.

'He can get up and get it himself,' was her only thought.

She was letting her bad morning affect her mood. And what was worse, she heard him chuckling.

The bacon was just about ready and time to start the scrambled eggs.

Distraction is a wonderful thing.

She got the pan nice and hot, pushed down the button to get the bread toasted, turned off the oven so the bacon didn't overcook and poured the eggs into the now hot pan. As the eggs started to do their thing she reached up and got two plates from the cupboard.

Out of the corner of her eye she saw him dispose of his empty juice glass in the sink and pour himself another cup of coffee. All while smiling at her.

He's always so upbeat, except of course when he's irritated with her. 'Right back at you, Fifty!' she yelled in her head.

'Focus, Becs,' she scolded herself, 'you have eggs to scramble.'

Without a word he was behind her when the toast popped and he grabbed both pieces and put one on each plate giving her a quick peck on the cheek as he did.

Way to defuse the situation and make her blush all at the same time. Well played, Mr Curtis.

Eggs done, pan off and she carefully pulled the bacon out and deposited the six slices on the waiting paper towel letting them drain the little bit of fat.

Pleased with herself and thinking, 'this is why you buy center cut… more meat less fat.'

She scooped up two thirds of the eggs and four slices of bacon onto one plate and the rest on to the second plate. He wasn't surprised in the least when she handed him the larger of the two portions. And took her seat across from him.

He cordially added, "Thank you. Looks delicious and I do expect you to eat everything on your plate since you chose your portion size."

'Does he now?'

She was thinking she should really loan him her books… but on second thoughts, hell no!

They ate in silence for a few minutes and each reached for the hot sauce at the same time.

It's the funny little things you seem to remember in something so generic as breakfast. And she liked that they had something so blasé as hot sauce on eggs in common.

With a wave, and 'ladies first' remark he rose and headed to the fridge looking for jam apparently. Success!

Thank goodness she remembered to get some on her shopping expedition. Pat on the back for making a list.

As he applied jam to his toast, he took notice that her toast hadn't been touched and was off to the side of her placemat and no longer on her plate. He reached over and placed it back on her plate and shook his head. "All of your breakfast, Becca, remember."

'Oh, for crying out loud,' she thought. She'd already eaten over half her eggs and a whole slice of bacon plus the yogurt, orange juice and peanut butter. Way more food than she usually eats in the morning or all of yesterday.

That is something he must never know.

Her stubbornness coming out, she made the conscious choice of not eating the toast and staring right at him, removed it again from her plate and was tempted to drop it on the floor but resisted the urge. Probably a good thing since this seemed to be a bone of contention with him. And his threat was still in her thoughts.

Out of the pages of a book.

He didn't look happy and to try and appease him, she picked up the remaining piece of bacon and took a large bite.

He shook his head. "You are a very taxing woman I must say, but I'll let the toast slide, this time."

And with that he continued to finish his breakfast as did she, minus toast.

Small victory in her mind.

Now to address the elephant in the room.

She was getting the dish soap out and preparing to clean up when she turned and looked over at him. He was watching her every move, again. She wasn't sure why she liked that so much.

'It's now or never,' she thought… "So, I was thinking now that we've eaten, and I'm feeling perfectly fine… maybe I don't need to be supervised every minute of the day. I'm sure you have better things to do on the lake, what with your shakedown cruise and all, plus I'm used to doing my own thing for the better part of the day. How about we compromise and you come back around five or six and pick me up for dinner instead?"

This fulfilled two things in her mind. She wasn't going to get hijacked onto the yacht for the next week or so and it would be a second date in one day.

Even mad… she had to admit, she liked having him around.

He stood and started to clear the plates and handed them to her. He then put the jam and hot sauce back into the fridge.

She started the hot water and added soap and a bit of bleach since she washed in lake water. She had just put her hands into the soapy water when he wrapped his arms around her waist placing his chin on the top of her head. She leaned back into his shoulder and he sighed. "What do you do here all day by yourself that you can't do with me on the yacht? I have seen you swim and to tell you the truth, I don't like you doing that with no one around. You also go into the woods alone; not a fan of that one either. What would happen if you got hurt? And then there is the very apparent fact that you don't eat enough; especially, with all the energy you expel throughout your day. So, my counter proposal is that I spend the day here with you and you come out to the yacht with me this evening for dinner and before you ask, yes, you'll be spending the night in my bed." And with that he kissed the top of her head and let her go with a quick slap on her ass and headed into the living room.

That remark, that slap stirred up some feelings she hadn't experienced in a very long time. Years in fact. And she was sure she was blushing, again. But at least she was facing towards the sink so no one could see.

She finished doing the dishes all while trying to catch her breath and steady her pulse.

Damn, where did this man come from? What did he mean his bed?

Well, let's not get ahead of ourselves. Maybe he was planning on sleeping somewhere else.

Was she ready for any amount of intimacy? She didn't think so.

She wasn't even mad about the swimming remark... even though she'd been swimming in this lake, her lake, since she was two years old. And how is he seeing her swim and hike? It's not like that huge boat can hide. She was a bit flattered all the same. He was like her personal guardian angel.

Wiping down the table and stove and putting the toaster away gave her some sort of normalcy during her thought process. Might as well make the bed too. Which made her blush again.

There sitting on her bed was her bag all packed, by the beautiful man in the other room, currently stoking the fire. She moved it off to the side and tugged the sheets back into place, then the light blanket and finally the bedspread. Fluff up the pillows and one more task completed.

She needed to take her meds but noticed they were missing from the bedside table. He must have packed them... damn, he really was serious.

She reached back over, grabbed the bag and opened it up to find it thoroughly packed with jeans, shorts, shirts, underwear... hell... even her flannel shirt was in there... and there were her meds.

She grabbed the pill caddy and turned right into him. Her squeal made him laugh.

"Christ, Cain, you're very stealthy," and she smacked his chest. His smile never diminished as he handed her a glass of water.

How does he do that?

She needed to remove him from the bedroom; it made her very nervous so she walked back into the kitchen and he followed.

Good.

Now what?

Still too early to swim or to even take a walk in the woods. The sun was barely up.

What she really wanted to do was lie down and take a nap. It's been one hell of a morning. And her hand was hurting, probably shouldn't have put it in the hot water... bandages don't like water. It's now in the trash. Maybe she should put more ointment on it.

She was actually cranky now.

She didn't want a babysitter or to have to entertain her guest either… she didn't have the energy.

Mr Psychic again picking up on her vibe, mood or facial expression because he knew exactly what she was thinking. His intuition was amazing and a tad scary.

"Come on, you're tired. Let's put you back to bed for a couple hours." She didn't even attempt to argue. It's what she wanted to do anyway.

His arm came around her waist as he led her into the bedroom. He pulled back the bedspread only and she crawled underneath. He closed the blinds to take away the little light there was and then put her bag on the floor and to her surprise laid down next to her folding her into his arms.

Kissing her forehead, he simply said, "Go to sleep, baby," and she did just that.

When she woke the clock read twenty after one… oh wow… she did sleep. Better than she had in a very long time. His arm was still around her, they were spooning. And she felt safe and warm. She was tempted to close her eyes and stay right there for the rest of the day but she really had to pee.

Reality seems to find a way to take special moments away.

And she almost laughed at the thought.

Now, how to move as to not disturb him.

She went to lift his arm and it came tighter around her and she knew then he was awake.

"Good afternoon, Becca, sleep well, I hope? I know I did."

That made her blush, again. "Yes, very well. Best in quite some time actually. Thank you for staying with me, Cain."

His grip tightened even more and he kissed the back of her head. "Nowhere else I'd rather be, baby."

That made her smile but his grip made her realize how bad she needed the bathroom.

"I need to get up please. Nature calls."

He tightened up his grip even more, which she didn't think was possible. And without missing a beat, "you know that a full bladder makes for a more intense orgasm?"

Her whole body tensed. 'What?'

He released his hold on her and got up chuckling to himself.

So not funny, she thought as she bolted for the bathroom.

He was still grinning like the Cheshire cat when she emerged.

He knew he threw her for a loop with that remark and she figured that was his hope.

Get her thinking about what comes next.

She smiled to herself since they did just sleep together.

Totally moving off that subject, she wondered if he'd like to take a swim.

He was thinking about something a tad different apparently.

"So, I leave for Alaska at the end of next week and I was thinking you should come with me."

'SAY what?'

"You don't have to answer right now but please will you at least think about it?"

She nodded because that's all she could do at that moment in time. He never ceased to amaze her. Shock her even.

She headed out to the deck to retrieve her suit... she really needed a swim to clear her mind now.

It was almost like she was on autopilot when she noticed him staring at her like she had completely lost her mind.

Her expression must be one of utter disbelief because that is where her mind was currently residing.

Had he really just asked her to travel with him... to Alaska...WOW!

He stopped her and took her face into his hands. Leaning slightly, he tilted her head up to meet his and put his lips on hers. Tenderly he kissed her and then his tongue found an opening and captured hers.

Oh my.

His hands left her face and traveled down her body pulling her body closer to his and a moan escaped from her mouth to his, mid kiss. This fueled their kisses' intensity. Her body was coming alive again under this man's touch and she found that frightening.

She didn't realize that she was shaking until he pulled away, looking down with confused and concerned eyes.

He probably thought she was having a blood sugar issue or a seizure… truth was, in her experience as soon as a man got laid, he was gone and the one that did stick around told her that she was the worst lay he'd ever had and she was terrified of Cain finding out that dirty little secret. She had many but that one was in the forefront at this moment in time.

Being told how bad you are in bed is not something a woman forgets. Plus, it had been well over a decade since she even had intercourse.

'He needed to go find someone else.'

Holding her hands, he asked, "What's going on in that head of yours? I'm fine hearing the word no or stop but your reaction goes way beyond that. First off, your body was giving me all the signs that you were enjoying yourself as much as I was and secondly, we were just kissing, Becca."

She was so embarrassed and still had no idea what she should tell him. The truth made her sound pathetic and she didn't want it to be some sort of challenge that he had to rise to, literally.

It was just a kiss… a very good and arousing… knee- buckling kiss. But still a kiss all the same.

He raised his eyebrow and she sighed. 'I think I'm beginning to really like this man.'

Another confession... well shit! She couldn't even look him in the eye but was looking down at her feet when she told him, "It's just been a very long time since someone has kissed me in a way that made me feel, well anything. I wasn't prepared to have that reaction to your kiss. You might say I'm out of practice and the thought does terrify me. I'm sorry but you should go find someone else. I'm damaged goods." She wanted to leave but his arms were around her before she could even turn.

"Baby, don't you ever be sorry about telling me what you're thinking or feeling. And I like who I found already. We'll take it as slow as you need. But just so you know... I enjoyed kissing you and I would like to do that a lot more. And, another thing, I'm not going anywhere, so you might want to get used to having me around. Now, out of curiosity... how long has it been? And seriously, I have wanted you since you walked down the stairs with coffee the first time, trying not to trip." She could hear the smile in his voice.

That last comment floored her. She never considered herself sexual or imagined anyone desiring her. Her blush deepened.

She hugged him harder to let him know how much that statement meant to her.

He kissed the top of her head.

She shielded her face again, talking into his chest, as she told him how long she'd been chaste. "It's not something I'm comfortable talking about but it's been around fourteen years, give or take." She heard him almost gasp. "Truth is, I was informed I was more work than it was worth and that I wasn't very good in bed anyway. "She really wanted to crawl into a hole after admitting that morsel. But his arms tightened around her like a blanket.

She could feel the tension surging through him and it scared her a bit.

Maybe he would be leaving after all.

Her husband could be cruel when he drank, which he did a lot in the early years of their marriage and when he got sober, they never had any intimate relations; one reason was his health, the other was her distain for his comments and how she felt about herself. He couldn't remember all the things he said and she could never forget.

When Cain lessened his hold on her, she saw that he looked utterly shocked and taken aback by her remark and was now staring down at her saddened face.

Back into another hug he whispered into her ear, "Oh my sweet baby, that isn't right on any level. I have no idea who hurt you like that and made you feel unwanted but it wasn't me. And I lied before… we're not taking this slow anymore. I am going to show you just how much I desire you."

He released her and took her hand leading her into the bedroom and closing the door behind them.

She was ever so happy he did too!

The clock read just after four when she woke and the sun was high in the sky. She was laying on her stomach looking out the bedroom window and listening to his steady breathing... it was one of the most beautiful sounds.

He needed his rest; he'd been quite busy for the past couple of hours.

She could still feel his lips, his fingers, his tongue all over her body. It was beyond anything she'd ever experienced before. She never knew one person could have that many orgasms. But she just did.

As she looked over the lake, another quote from the same favorite movie as earlier in the day popped into her thoughts, 'we did things that would frighten fish'. It made her laugh out loud.

His hand reached over and cupped her left butt cheek and gave it a squeeze. Then her right before turning her over so he could see her face.

"What's so funny, baby?"

She told him and he laughed too but his was more wicked in nature. And that look.

"Woman, I love your wit. But can I ask you something?" She nodded. "Why did you ask me if I was leaving after we had sex the first time?" She cringed. When he told her 'hell no' her surge of relief was very visible at least to her.

Not waiting for a response his lips came forcefully onto hers and his tongue took command of her mouth. Her body responded in kind and she could feel his erection. He was a force.

She was already quite sore from earlier and she wondered where this man's stamina came from but wished he could bottle it... and damn it, she needed to pee.

She didn't want to stop him, it felt so amazing and his attention to her breasts was arousing her beyond belief.

When she moved away, he stopped her, asking where she thought she was going.

"I have to pee."

That wicked grin was back with a vengeance... "Really?" And with that he pulled her back and retook command of her lips and breasts. His exuberance was infectious and if anyone asks... multiple orgasms with full bladders are indeed intense. Thank you very much.

They laid there in each other's arms, sated and happy.

He didn't have to work very hard to get her body to do whatever he wanted. And his body reacted to hers in much the same way. Maybe she wasn't a bad lover after all. That thought made her quite joyful.

He finally broke the silence. "Baby, I can lay here all night long with you, but you have very little food in your refrigerator and you need to eat and so do I. So, let's get dressed and head out to the yacht for supper. Then depending how sore I've already made you we might just need to christen my bed on the yacht later tonight." And with a playful smack on her bare ass he was up.

She gasped.
Oh my!
More!

TGIF (THANK GOD IT'S FRIDAY)

She was naked as a jaybird under the sheet in his massive oversized bed and wondered if there was a robe or something to put on before she got up. Her bag was somewhere but she didn't see it in the stateroom.

Since they were sharing the sheet, she didn't think he would appreciate her removing it. Although the thought did occur to her.

She admonished herself, 'grow up' and got out of bed and headed into the bathroom. She almost screamed when she started peeing... it stung. Bad. But it felt oh so good getting there... she blushed at the thought.

What an astounding lover Cain was... but damn, he never seemed to get enough, did she?

The thought of him made her whole body come alive. Even now. 'Fuck.'

She glanced in the mirror... her hair was a fright... beyond bed head. She needed her brush and clothes.

He was awake and watching her as she climbed back under the sheet. She was still very self-conscious of her body.

Excess body actually. Her legs were fabulous, but her middle was a tab squishy.

He pulled her back into his front so they were spooning. His hand against her tummy. The one part of her body she hated.

He breathed into ear, "Baby, I love that you have a little meat on your bones. It gives me something to hold, squeeze and fondle... so don't you ever be ashamed of it... you're beautiful and I love kissing every inch of you... if you hadn't already noticed. There is nothing I don't find sexy and voluptuous about you. If you don't believe me, we can spend the entire day in this bed where I can show you just how much you turn me on... again and again."

She brought his hand to her lips and kissed every finger and his palm before she spoke. "Thank you, my love. I do believe you and since I'm already quite sore, maybe we could find another activity you might enjoy, skeet shooting perhaps?"

He chuckled at her suggested activity and with a more astonished tone, "Sore, I am amazed you could walk." He was grinning. "I'm trying to make up for fourteen years here. I figure I still owe you, roughly one thousand two hundred more climaxes to get you back on track. Don't misunderstand, I'm looking forward to each and every one of them. And one more thing, you calling me 'my love' is like music to my ears." He kissed her cheek.

She turned to look him in the eye. "Okay, that explains a lot. I was beginning to think you were a sex maniac. Not that I'm complaining mind you... but you don't owe me anything. And I sure as hell didn't tell you so you would take it as some mantle you needed to run with. You didn't even know me then. I am happy just being with you now. There is no need for it to be anything else than what it is."

That grin… that insatiable mouth. Those lips and the kiss that told it all… he wasn't backing down… and with a breathy whisper… "sore be damned, baby… and it's not keeping score as much as putting a wrong… right. I think we'll try for a twofer this morning."

The lord's name was used several times in vain that morning by them both.

She was famished when breakfast was served and she started to make good headway on her ham, cheese and mushroom omelet. Cain had a healthy appetite as well from that morning's physical exertion but seemed content watching her eat.

'Freak!'

Just over halfway through the wonderful meal that was set before her, her stomach started to grumble causing her to make a mad dash to the back bathroom, just in time before giving her repast back to the porcelain gods.

Food wasn't her friend some days and she felt very embarrassed. Plus, she couldn't find her toothbrush, but her bag was sitting on the bench in the bathroom. She wondered where it came from.

She made the conscious choice to use Cain's since she knew where his mouth had been the past two hours.

Yep, that thought brought on a nice shade of pink to her skin.

She looked up mid-brush to see Cain standing behind her shaking his head.

"Mi casa es su casa, sweetheart. And Joel made you a protein shake."

Even though she'd just brushed her teeth she felt compelled to try the shake since her stomach made a growl.

Man, did Joel know what he was doing; it tasted amazing.

They were sitting on the bed when Cain told her all about his chef.

As it turns out Joel Warren was also a nutritionist and had informed Cain, he knew how to help Becca eat the right foods to help with her low diabetic numbers as well as what she should be eating so she wouldn't continue to get sick.

It wasn't the omelet that made her ill per se, but the fact that she would eat such small amount at one sitting.

He noticed at dinner that she only ate a small portion of her steak and no potatoes.

Cain mentioned to him she liked protein drinks and a plan was made.

The frothy drink he made her had banana, peanut butter and almond milk along with some protein powder… it was very good and also very filling. She was relieved when Cain took it back with half still remaining, noting he didn't want her to get sick again.

She looked around and realized that the bed was made and the room looked like it had been vacuumed and tidied. She hadn't noticed that earlier when she sprinted into the bathroom.

But she was preoccupied.

Cain must have picked up on her curious look. "There is a staff on board that takes care of my needs and now all yours too. Their quarters are below deck and they are very good at their jobs and for the most part stay in the background."

He was trying the shake when a thought occurred to her.

"So, they're like the Oompa Loompas… just not orange, probably?"

Like his ability to scare her… she seemed to know when to say something totally off the wall while he was drinking something. Oops.

He managed not to spray the floor with protein shake but did have a bit of a coughing fit.

She did her best not to laugh but failed miserably.

Once he was able to contain the cough he could finally speak. "You have amazing timing with your comments."

Laughing can be infectious and he did join her in the amusing situation.

Once they were both composed, he continued, "I'll arrange for you to meet the entire staff before we head to Alaska. Now, how about you go pour us a bath…

you'll find the scented oils in the cupboard to the left of the shower. I'll join you in a few minutes."

He left her sitting on the bed staring at the stateroom door as he left closing it behind him.

Did he think she hadn't heard the Alaska comment? That trip hadn't been determined and she needed to attend to her home in northeastern Nevada. Not to mention pay her bills.

Life seems to get in the way of what seemed like an utter fantasy to her.

To the task at hand.

The tub was huge and jetted. *The whole stateroom and bathroom were bigger than her cabin. He designed it very well.*

She'd never seen that many jets in a tub before and she could tell it was custom made. It was deeper and wider than most and the waterfall faucet made short work of filling it up. She chose lavender and vanilla foaming bath beads from the array of oils and scents she found in the cupboard. Too many for a stud like Cain. A woman had to pick these out.

He must have a woman in every town he visits... how could he not? With his stamina he should have two. She shook her head.

She caught movement out of the corner of her eye so he didn't startle her that time. His being naked did... which was silly since she just poured a tub.

He walked over and made quick work of her clothing and helped her step into the massive thing. He

71

followed with a smirk that made her curious and nervous at the same time.

The Cheshire cat would have been impressed with his grin. Then he asked her if she was ready for the jets. She nodded and every jet came to life.

Holy crap… they were everywhere and hit her in places that she wasn't sure jets should.

He moved her around so he could control two of the jets hitting her clitoris and vagina. She tried to move but he told her to be still. He then started blocking and unblocking the jets arousing every fiber of her being. She was stunned that the jets made such short work giving her a very violent orgasm with aftershocks, but Cain wasn't done and unblocked their full power as he held her in such a position she couldn't move and the jets kept pulsing everywhere. His lips were keeping her girls very happy. She had lost count and was on the verge of yet another one before she was so overly aroused, she had to beg him to turn them off. She was still feeling the effects of the jets when he pulled her around to face him.

He seemed quite pleased with himself.

"Put your legs around my waist so I can have you, baby."

He was fully erect and as she did as he requested, he buried himself deep inside her.

She was so overly stimulated that he generated yet another orgasm and she felt minor tremors until his release. That made up for two years she thought.

His arms were wrapped about her as they both caught their breath. He was kissing her lips very gently and asked if she was okay?

She nodded not finding any words yet.

Had he designed the tub with that in mind or was it just a thought when he decided on a bath that morning?

"So, I hope you had as much fun as I did? We just christened the tub and I'm so glad I put in those extra jets now." He was indeed quite pleased with himself.

She wasn't sure how she felt; other than, thoroughly fucked. It was intense and she wondered if she'd be able to walk now. She thought maybe she was too old for this kind of sexual activity. What was she at now, forty or fifty orgasms in less than twenty-four hours? Too many to count, that was for sure. Okay, nine... still... A LOT!

She finally found her voice as he pulled her onto his lap and started to caress her hair looking a bit concerned that she'd not spoken for quite some time.

"I'm not sure I'll survive one thousand one hundred more of those. What an obit that would be, death by orgasm."

He started to laugh. And without missing a beat let her know that he knew CPR.

Of course, he did.

He also corrected her number to one thousand one hundred and ninety-five.

He helped her on her feet and out of the tub directing her to the shower.

A walk-in shower that would fit at least four people comfortably with an oversized rain head.

He was draining the tub before taking her hand and leading her into the shower. He got the temperature perfect and proceeded to wash her hair and every inch of her body... it was heavenly. She kindly returned the favor.

They wrapped in oversize towels and he handed her a smaller towel for her hair, which she made look like a turban as they went back in the bedroom.

She looked again but couldn't find her toiletry bag so no lotion or antiperspirant or perfume. She already knew her brush wasn't there. And since Cain didn't have hair... on his head, he didn't have one to borrow.

She was sitting on the ottoman by the big leather chair in the corner thinking about asking to go back to the cabin where all her stuff was, including a blow dryer.

He walked out of his closet wearing jeans, a white button up shirt and brown leather deck shoes. So frickin' hot.

"What's wrong? You're not dressed. I thought we'd go into town and do a bit of shopping if you're game. We both are going to need a few things for Alaska. And I would like to buy you some new lingerie, if you'll let me."

Such a hopeful request.

She faked being appalled. "What, you don't like my sexy over-sized shorts and tank top? Well, I never." He didn't play fair. "I like you out of them better."

She couldn't help but smile and blush. But continued, "Truth is, I don't have a few things I need from the cabin. And I hate shopping, well not so much shopping as all the people, just so you know."

It dawned on him in two seconds when looking at the towel on her head.

"CRAP, I forgot to pack your bathroom. I'm so sorry. Okay, get dressed. We'll stop by the cabin on the way up to your car."

She knew she didn't have a choice but decided that during their forty-minute drive to town they would be chatting about Alaska.

Dressed in jeans and her favorite cold shoulder top, they boarded the launch to head for the cabin. He handed her a lifejacket which she held but refused to put on... hell they were close enough she could just swim.

Her hair was as dry as she could get it with a towel but fingers aren't a good brush.

Less than five minutes and they were docked and heading up the cabin stairs hand in hand. It felt right and wrong to her.

Once inside she headed to get a few personal matters taken care of and felt much better when she came out of the bathroom with totally dry hair and wearing her favorite perfume.

"Damn, woman, you smell good enough to eat. But we'll address that later. Time to shop. Can I drive please?"

As she blushed from his forward remark, she handed him her keys and they headed to the top of the hill.

Once there he looked down the hill and asked why she didn't back down. She 'fessed up that it made her nervous and the walk up was good for her. He just shook his head as he opened the passenger door for her.

He started the Buick and off they went. She was glad she filled the tank before she left town… some guys have a thing about that.

It's amazing where the mind goes sometimes. She had to laugh at herself.

Before entering the main road that led to the highway he turned and asked where the best shopping would be.

She told him the city of Spokane would, but it was a ninety-five-minute drive each way as opposed to the forty minutes to town. He nodded and off they went towards the highway.

Now the big topic and the bigger question… did she want to go with him to the forty-ninth state? YES, who wouldn't.

ALASKA — She wasn't sure how to approach the subject since they weren't exactly talking about it so she decided to go around the issue. Why was she so nervous…? 'Stop being a wimp, Becs.'

"I'll be needing to head home in a week or so and get my bills paid and make sure my house is still standing. So, I was thinking maybe I could fly up and meet you in Alaska in Ketchikan maybe." She Googled the closest airport in the state.

She liked her compromise idea and glad it came to her that morning so she could use the internet to help solve the minor dilemma. He had to see her reasoning.

Or not!

He countered, "Better yet, I'll help you set up autopay on all your bills, which really you should have done years ago. Seriously, Becca, you still write checks? That's archaic in this day and age. As for your property worries, we'll hire a caretaker and I will be happy to cover the cost. We sail from Seattle in roughly eight days. And I want you aboard for the whole experience. Should be quite the trip."

Sweet and infuriating. Not to mention just a wee bit bossy.

"Listen, Fifty, I do not need you setting up anything for me." And folded her arms totally pissed.

Well that confused him a tad. On a couple of levels.

"I'm forty-three not fifty so I don't get the reference and I am sure you're more than capable. But you haven't so I just offered to help. What are you mad about?"

She couldn't help but laugh… she knew he wouldn't get the nickname.

He shook his head and she knew she might want to explain. "The reference is from a book… you remind me a bit of the main character that's all. And for being mad, you're being a bit presumptuous since I never actually said I would go to Alaska."

He pulled over. Oh, that's not good.

"Yes, you did… this morning in bed I asked you to please come with me on the trip and you said yes. And what book?"

Sex… REALLY!

Oh, for the love of God. "YOU asked during sex when I probably would have confessed to killing JFK and since I was four years from actually being born… it was quite a feat. I'm amazed the papers got it all wrong. And the book is called Fifty Shades."

He started to laugh. "Damn, woman, I really do love your wit." And with that she couldn't help but join in the laughter…bad mood averted.

Finally composed and back on the road he seemed deep in thought. She wondered what he could be thinking about.

They made it to the highway and he turned left, really… they were shopping in Spokane.

'Aw shit!'

He finally revealed what he'd been thinking about. "That was a chick flick right… rich guy banging some young thing in a sex room?" She nodded and thought his explanation was very fitting. "I don't see the connection except maybe you thought the jets were a bit of a violation. If that is the case I apologize."

She did and didn't but that's not even close to the reason she called him 'Fifty'.

"That's not why. And for the most part I very much enjoyed the jets, thank you."

He was smiling her favorite smile.

When she was honest with herself, she really did want to go to Alaska so maybe she'd let him help her set up autopay. But first he needed to sweat a little.

She closed her eyes for a moment to reflect.

He woke her with a lovely kiss. "Hey, beautiful, we're here. Time to shop. And I still want to know why 'Fifty' is a suitable nickname for me."

She stretched and gave him a kiss back. She then looked for her purse but it was nowhere to be found. Did she even bring it? Well hell.

"What are you looking for?" Holding out his hand to her.

"Purse, but I don't remember if I brought it." He shook his head letting her know she hadn't.

She didn't want to shop but what if she found something... now she couldn't buy anything. That made her a bit sullen.

A very easy expression to read.

"If you see anything you want just let me know and I'll buy it for you. It would be my distinct pleasure."

She asked if she could pay him back and he gave her a resounding 'no'.

She took his hand as they walked in the mall deciding then and there that she wouldn't want or need anything.

She could be stubborn. But then again... so could he.

Mr Mind reader strikes again. "Becca, if you see something you want, I really want to buy it for you. I'll take it in trade if that makes you happy." And patted her ass.

Huge blush!

First stop was Victoria's Secret... she loathed this store... it was designed for skinny bitches and she couldn't think of one reason they needed to go in there.

She didn't have to wait long.

The size two salesgirl was bubbly and all too eager to assist Cain, who took the whole situation in his stride. His response to 'how can I help you?'... nearly floored Becca.

"We're looking for new bra and panty sets for my girlfriend. She'll need to be measured to get the right fit and the sexier the better."

She looked at him like he'd grown two heads. Her thoughts were more like... hell, no we are not. Go get yourself measured.

"Please don't be difficult about this. You've obviously lost quite a bit of weight since nothing you have fits you and all you seem to own is boy shorts." That damn smile, those piercing eyes.

Fuck it!

She followed the overly attentive girl to the fitting room.

Once alone with the young woman she asked if she could just try on a few to see what fits without the precise numbers. Apparently, that's not how it's done and her mood soured instantly.

She had indeed dropped a few sizes which bettered her demeanor but Cain was having way too much fun picking out different items for her to try on and of course wanted to see them. Not awkward at all.

'This day sucks.'

Finally, a bra he liked and it had matching panties he deemed sexy enough. She liked them too but was really tired of trying things on so she was hoping she was done.

She wanted coffee. Cain had other ideas.

Next on his list... Nightgowns... baby doll... but at least she only had to try on two.

They were pretty... the black one was cotton, fitted and very sheer. She shook her head when she saw the price for very little material. The pink one was satin and had embroidered panels on either side from basically under her arm to well above her knee and neither side left much to the imagination. Oh my.

And before you ask... yes, he came right in the dressing room to look and approved both.

His fingers explored both sides of the embroidery on the sheer pink one which made Becca squirm.

"Baby, if we weren't in a dressing room right now." And with that evocative tidbit he left her alone to get her heart back to a normal sinus rhythm.

Damn that man!

When she emerged from the dressing room, he was at checkout with many more items than she thought were necessary.

She didn't want to seem totally ungrateful but he didn't need to break the bank on bras either. Keeping her voice low, "I think you are going way overboard. I don't need all that. Can we please just compromise and only get one or two items? Please."

He kept his voice as low as she did. "Nope, you need panties for at least a week and matching bras makes the set. You knew I was getting the nightgowns and I grabbed you two new robes along with a couple other things which you can model for me once we're in private. I want to buy you these so, stop with anymore protests."

The salesgirl, yep the same size two, looked up from entering all his purchases and without missing a beat let them know the total was $982.

She gasped. Cain took her hand and ever so slightly squeezed it with a small shake of his head. Then handed the girl his platinum card.

Becca knew that she'd just been scolded for her reaction.

She wanted her keys back. He could find another way home. He was being high-handed again and it was annoying the crap out of her.

She closed her eyes, took a cleansing breath and focused. "Thank you so much for the lovely lingerie, sweetheart, you shouldn't have." That should have enough saccharine in it... even for Cain. She also followed it with a smile and squeezed his hand back.

Man, did he see right through her.

With his eyebrow up and an evil grin... she knew he was plotting some sort of revenge.

She needed to try and defuse the situation which he had caused and she may have overreacted to, a tab. But either way she needed to make up with him and avoid his possible wrath.

As they walked out the store he asked, "How about a coffee?"

"Oh yes please, thank you. "That made her happy and she sounded it.

"So, coffee is okay and you sound appreciative but a few pieces of cloth and it's like I committed some serious infraction. You are an enigma." He concluded with, "And unlike any woman I've ever known."

That made her feel horrible and happy; she didn't like to conform to what everyone else would do, and of course now she wondered how many women are we talking about. Does he take them all shopping? Maybe that's his thing.

She also knew she needed to respond but her brain was suddenly tired and she was quite hungry too.

Those two go hand in hand when you don't eat a lot.

The third tell to low sugar levels is getting a bit bitchy. TRIFECTA!

She offered to carry one of the two bags but he refused so she took possession of his other hand as they walked down the mall towards Starbucks.

She finally brought his hand up to her lips and gently kissed it. "I'm sorry. And thank you for the lovely pieces of cloth. It was way too generous but so very sweet. And if I may impose on your generosity again, I'm very hungry so maybe you will buy me lunch?"

He stopped and looked at her with the most adoring smile that lit up his whole face. "It would be my honor to escort you to lunch. Thank you for asking and for letting me know that you need food."

And with that, coffee went on hold and they headed to the food court.

Not exactly the romantic atmosphere you might want but at least you have lots of choices.

They both headed to Subway without even asking each other.

Again, it's the little things that make you smile and for some, weird reason, that did.

She ate every bite of her salad while Cain managed to woof down a foot-long sub with double meat.

Well, they both had exerted quite of bit of energy the past twenty-four hours.

Lunch done, back to the task at hand... more shopping.

But this time he was looking for them both.

"We are going to need a jacket and some attire for sailing on Alaskan waters." She grinned and nodded in approval and that made him come to a dead stop as they entered Macy's.

He sounded like a kid at Christmas. "You're coming with me? No side trips needed?"

"Nope... but you'll have to help me set up the autopay and I'll have friends extend the mail hold and look in on my place while we're away."

She found herself wrapped in his big arms with his lips by her ear so only she could hear him. "Baby, I so want to jump you right now." Her blush however was seen by anyone walking by.

That smile never left his face while picking out one light jacket for each of them and one heavier one. He also insisted on getting them both a few long sleeve shirts. No dressing rooms required. Small favors.

Back in the mall they walked hand in hand to Starbucks, final stop before home she hoped.

He handed her twenty dollars and asked her to order him a macchiato with an extra shot. He needed to run into Barnes and Noble for the newest Forbes magazine and asked if she needed a new book or anything. She declined.

He was back just as they called her name, letting her know that her order was ready, perfect timing.

While she doctored her iced coffee, he consolidated their purchases into three bags that he could easily carry with one hand, picked up his coffee with the other and they headed back to the car.

"So, home now?" she asked quite optimistically.

"Not yet... only one more stop to make though. "His smile was wicked again.

He drove less than two miles and pulled into the parking lot in front of an adult toy store. 'Holy crap, batman' and she turned a wonderful shade of crimson. As he came around to open her door for her, she locked it. He was laughing pretty hard when he hit the key fob and unlocked and opened the door taking her hand.

"Don't tell me you've never been in one or owned a vibrator. Besides we're just looking around." And with that, they walked into the store.

She didn't want to touch many items since some looked downright scary and others looked like they would hurt.

She did stop and read about one of the newest vibrators called 'the Grey'. She was blushing again when he came up behind her and scared the crap out her.

"I already grabbed that one. It seemed fitting since you've chosen my new nickname, which you still haven't explained. Plus, I got some Ben-Wa balls, handcuffs and was thinking about butt plugs or anal beads... you game?"

Like a kid in a candy store.

She shook her head. "You first," and with that she headed to the door. She heard the car door click to let her know he'd unlocked it for her.

Good man.

The drive back to the lake was a bit quiet in the beginning. She didn't know if he was miffed at her exit and he also seemed to be thinking about something pretty hard.

She broke the silence this time. "What has you so deep in thought?"

They were on the highway now so he didn't look at her. "I need to work tomorrow for a few hours and after I thought we'd set up your auto payments if that is okay with you?"

"Sure. Of course. While you're occupied, I can make all of my other arrangements and tidy up the cabin." He nodded but his demeanor was still off.

Maybe she was too old for relationships. All she really wanted to do was hit him upside his head and yell 'spill it' for fuck sake. She chose to just stare out the window and ignore him.

"Becca, how many men have you slept with?" Well that came out of nowhere and managed to garner a jump and a little surprise gasp.

He made apologies but his Cheshire grin didn't fool anyone.

'So that's what he's been thinking about.' Okay then.

"Four, including you. What about you?" 'Good girl,' she thought to herself.

"A lot more than four. But I wanted you to know… you're the first in well over a year. And you're the only one ever on my boat."

She smiled and felt very lucky to have met this wonderful, amazing man.

But was surprised he hadn't been with anyone for sixteen months.

"Those past men… were one-night stands? Well the first two anyway, you married the third." He was bringing up a topic that made her insides hurt.

She wasn't proud that she let herself get picked up in a bar, when all women look like Bo Derek at closing time.

She nodded.

He took her hand and brought it to his lips. "They left as soon as they got off, leaving you feeling horrible, right." She nodded again wondering where he was going with this.

"I'm thinking we should start you over. Reboot your sexual encounters. I think I am your first true lover." She treasured that idea and nodded again but this time with a very thankful smile. The pain left her eyes.

That made her realize all the more just how very naive she was when it came to sex and he was extraordinarily gifted. And she really wanted to ask him a few questions.

Although she was horribly embarrassed, she thought it might be easier with him driving and not being able to see her blushing through the entire process.

Bucking up the nerve, 'In the end, communication is everything, Becs!'

Now where to start this whole ordeal. From the beginning 'you idiot'. She was very good at chastising herself.

"Cain, can I ask you a few things... about sex?"

His face was looking a tab amused but nodded to let her know to continue.

"You're incredibly good at oral sex and I was wondering if you would teach me the nuances of pleasuring you that way? I was told long ago how bad I was at it and I can't have that when it comes to you? Reboot and all."

The SUV swerved as Cain was trying to control his anger. She just wasn't sure who he was mad at.

"Becca, I don't and can't believe that you're bad at anything when it comes to sex. You've impressed the crap out of me already on several levels but yes, I will tell you what feels good when we get to that. We just aren't there yet and as you so amply said earlier, you first."

"Now, is there anything else?"

"Why are you mad at me?"

"Baby, I'm not, I'm sorry... it's just that you've been hurt so deeply and told lies that you believe and that

89

angers me to the core. Not at you but the fucking idiot who said them. But I really do want to answer any questions or concerns you might have so please, continue."

She looked out the side window wondering if she should ask, but it can't hurt... right.

"I was wondering if you liked spanking? The couple of times you've playfully smacked my ass was exciting. I wondered if you'd spank me?"

"Becca, honey I would love to but we are going to have to finish this conversation when I'm not doing seventy-five miles an hour on the highway because you are making me hard and before you ask; no, now is not a moment you get to try your skills at helping in this situation."

After a couple of minutes he asked her to read an article out from the Forbes magazine he'd purchased earlier.

Well if that didn't change the mood nothing would. She was bored reading it but he seemed to be enjoying it... again, freak. His grin was priceless.

Once done with the reading she turned up the music and they both were quiet for the last twenty minutes of the drive. She figured he was concentrating on driving the dirt road to the cabin while she went back to relishing the idea of her getting her first sexual spanking.

She was beginning to really adore this man!

As he was backing the Enclave down the hill (show-off) he reminded her to pack her toiletry bag before they headed back for the yacht. She nodded.

She waited for him to open her door; he was quite chivalrous and smiled when he saw her waiting for him.

She took his hand as she stepped down and the next thing she knew she was up against the car with his lips parting hers with his ever eager tongue. His body was holding hers in place and they both started to moan. So much for concentrating on driving the last twenty minutes.

Again, note to self, 'sex talk while driving... not the worst idea.'

He finally released her mouth and put his to her ear. "Get your bag and get on the launch in two minutes or I'm going to take you on the dock. Now go." His voice was raspy as he tried to catch his breath and she could feel his erection and she knew better than to waste time.

He had the launch started and untied when she joined him. His look was primal. Once back to the boat, a young man was waiting to tie it up but she couldn't remember his name. She was going to ask Cain but his hand was waiting for hers and once on the platform he ushered her inside.

He leaned down to her ear once on the stairs and very sternly told her to get back to the stateroom and get out of her clothes and into bed. The quick smack on her ass got her moving.

She thought he was right behind her. He wasn't. In fact, she lay in bed for some time, quite some time since he woke her with soft kisses to both her eyelids, then her nose and finally her lips.

She smiled and looked up at him.

Something was different. He looked stern and she suddenly felt very underdressed.

He was standing by the bed now and informed her Joel would have dinner ready in less than half an hour. And with that he left her alone in his overly large stateroom with his massive custom-made bed.

She felt the cold and it wasn't from the temperature. And even though she'd bathed that morning she felt like she needed a quick shower.

Once dressed back in jeans and a fresh shirt she made her way to the salon that also housed the galley.

Her mood was concerning her since she could feel her heart starting to ache and that always brought on a darkness she would rather have happen in private. And alone... like utterly without people within one hundred miles.

Dinner smelled wonderful but her stomach was rolling and all she could think about was leaving. Thank goodness her cabin wasn't far. She could swim if she had to but that might tick him off.

When she looked out at the shoreline... Wait a minute... where was her cabin and for that matter... where was the fucking shoreline?

Cain startled her as he pulled out her chair. His smile was back but hers was now gone and she wasn't in the mood to fake it.

"We've moved, why?" She knew she sounded a bit too anxious.

Cain waited for Joel to set the food down in front of them both before he started to explain. "It was the reason I didn't join you earlier, which I'm very sorry about." Trying to gauge her nervous expression. "We got a warning from the sheriff's office to move the yacht to more open water since the weekends are much busier on that part of the lake. And as you mentioned the first time you saw her... she's a beast of a boat. And it's a process to store all the toys and get her moved and anchored up again."

She nodded.

He reached for her hand and asked her what was going on in that beautiful head of hers.

She couldn't answer with her heart crushing her every fiber of being.

She shook her head and picked up her fork in the hopes that would distract him. It did for the moment.

She managed a bite or two but really was just moving the food around on her plate.

"Baby, I want you to eat and I really want you to talk to me." He almost pleaded. "If you're mad about earlier, I am too and if it's about tomorrow, I'll have the 'kid' take you back to your cabin in the launch so you can swim and finish packing the rest of your belongings.

Or better yet, you can swim around the yacht and I'll take you Sunday." He was really trying to lighten her mood that was for sure.

She nodded and in a very quiet voice asked to be excused, saying she didn't feel well and just needed to lie down for a little bit.

His look of concern didn't go unnoticed but he pulled her chair out, gave her a quick kiss on her forehead and told her he'd be back to check on her in a little while.

The tears started before she reached her destination. The uncontrollable sobs hit as soon as she closed the door. She thought about locking the door for privacy but it wasn't her room. She so wished she was alone at the cabin. She always attributed these episodes as part of guilt more than sadness for a loss. She finally made her way to the big leather chair in the corner and brought her knees up to her chest, wrapping her arms around as best she could letting her heart release its agony and despair.

When Cain came in the room, she tried to hide her face; she knew she looked awful and this had nothing to do with him. Well not really.

He was having none of that and had her in his arms leading her to the bed where he cradled her and wrapped his arms around her like a security blanket bringing on another round of tears. He held her tighter and let the front of his shirt get soaked.

As he stroked her hair and kissed her head, she started to gain some control of the debilitating pain her heart released and the tears were almost manageable… she wanted a tissue.

With a very gallant and a bit unseemly move he pulled out the corner of his shirt and wiped her nose. That made her giggle and finally look at his very alarmed eyes. He kissed her tear-stained cheeks without releasing his grip.

They both jumped when there was a knock on the door. That made her smile. She tried to move but again he was having none of that.

"Yes?" with a slight edge to his voice.

It was Joel asking to enter with another smoothie for Miss Rebecca.

"Don't move, baby." He shifted her off his lap and went to the door, returning with a very purple-looking concoction.

He held out the glass for her to take and sat back on the bed. He had her back on his lap and wrapped his arms tightly around her once more. She loved that more than anything and took a drink and then another until it was gone. It was delicious and she must remember to thank Joel. Cain's smile was back. Her favorite and she kissed his lips saying thank you. Which covered a magnitude of things that night, the biggest was for not asking any questions.

SATURDAY and SUNDAY

When she woke, Cain wasn't in bed or anywhere in the stateroom. He had been so attentive the night before, she missed him… she also wondered where he came from and how did she get lucky enough to have him.

Smiling, she headed into the bath to get showered and dressed, checking the sky before she chose her attire… shorts, tank and sandals.

No one was in the salon but Joel was in the galley as usual.

He asked if she'd like something other than a smoothie and she did. The eggs and bacon were ready before she finished her first cup of coffee.

"Anything else I can get you, Miss Rebecca?" Joel was so very sweet.

But she needed to address this name thing now… she hated Rebecca.

She never thought she looked like a Rebecca… her mom named her Rebecca Lynne and she loved the name and was the only one that called her that. Her dad didn't care for it either so he always called her 'kitten'. She was grateful that didn't become her nickname. Her brother dubbed her Becca and that's the name that always stuck. Her best friend calls her Becs as does her young nephew and she likes that too. It's usually how she addresses herself.

"Joel, can you just call me Becca please. No need to be so formal. And thank you for a delicious breakfast and for the smoothie last night." She was hoping he would agree but they settled on 'Miss Becca' since Cain liked formal.

Of course, he did. So, fucking 'Fifty'.

She heard him this time so no surprise when his arms came around her as he kissed her cheek.

"Nice to see your appetite back. Did you want the kid to get the launch out for you today?"

He retrieved his arms and took the seat next to her as Joel handed him a cup of coffee.

She needed to solve the mystery. "What's the kid's name and no, I'll wait for you to take me tomorrow if you still want to?"

"Of course, I always want to take you." No double meaning there. She blushed and he grinned.

Joel answered her question. "His name is Kevin, he's actually the son of Captain Lawrence."

More talking to herself, she made the comment that he didn't look like a Kevin. Both Joel and Cain started to laugh.

Cain took her hand and kissed it. "That's why I call him kid. I've got to get back to work... why don't you explore the boat. This afternoon you can give me a fashion show of our purchases from yesterday." With a wink and quick kiss, he was heading to his study. Leaving her flush in more ways than one.

She knew the main deck pretty well: it had the salon which was the main living room, the galley, a dining area, a small back deck in the stern of the boat with a bistro table and chairs, a guest bathroom, Cain's study which might have been a guest bedroom on a different yacht, and of course, the enormous master stateroom so she headed up top to look around. On this level of the boat she found a nice gym, another bathroom, a very nice entertainment room with a TV you could probably see from space and seating for eight. On the back deck was a nice table and six chairs, wet bar and barbeque perfect for the swanky boat. That deck also housed two smaller guest rooms, one with its own en suite and further up in the bow were lounge chairs for catching a few rays, as well as bench seats on either side. The very top level was all bridge. One floor below the main deck were the crew's quarters, a second smaller galley and their private seating area, as well as another small back deck. She didn't stay long since she thought that was an intrusion in the crew's space. On the next lower level, she found the stored launch and four jet skis plus another deck that gave her access to the water via a swim step and a ladder to get back into the massive yacht. The very bottom level that was below the water line was all engine room and she didn't want to go down there. Damn this boat is HUGE!

On her way back up to the main salon she ran into the kid and asked if there was any problem with her going for a swim. He smiled and showed her where they kept the lifejackets and beach towels. Very nice and a tad confusing. She waved as she headed back to the main floor to change.

Back in the stateroom she grabbed her bathing suit and cover-up and went into the bathroom to change. Her cabin was all windows so it was a habit… she had to shake her head at herself. And the Oompa Loompa struck again… the room was made up to perfection.

She really must ask to meet the whole crew.

Cain's office door was shut so she knew he would be busy for another hour or two. Perfect time to get in a much-needed swim and to catch a few rays.

As stated earlier, she loved swimming in the late morning but also knew that the water out in the middle of the lake is much cooler than at the cabin.

Still she couldn't wait. She hadn't gotten to swim the last two days and she really missed it. Once she made her way down to the very back deck on the level above the engine room of the boat, she set her cover-up on the chair along with the towel she retrieved from the cabinet and jumped in.

"Wow, that's fucking cold," she gasped but she wasn't giving in. She made a small lap in the back on the boat and wondered how long it would take her to swim around the thirty-two-meter leviathan. And a small voice inside told her not to do it.

'Fine coward.'

She was acclimating to the temperature of the water and went off to the port side looking up, acknowledging just how big this thing was. She knew better than to swim too close since it was anchored and not docked. But there was no wind and little wake from other boats so she felt it was perfectly safe.

She wasn't expecting to be hit in the head by a lifejacket or seeing Cain on deck looking very cross. She grabbed the jacket and pushed it out in front of her as she swam to the back deck. She tossed the floatation item up onto the swim step where he was now standing and refused his hand when he tried to help her out of the water.

She walked past Cain, grabbed her towel and cover-up and headed up three decks to the lounge chairs she'd seen earlier. She never looked to see if he was following but, as she passed a very nervous Kevin, she knew that he must have gone and interrupted Cain to let him know of her impromptu swim. 'Nark!'

If looks could kill, that boy would be long gone.

She turned to find that Cain was indeed behind her looking miffed and pensive at the same time. She was just downright pissed and without caring about what he thought, told him, "I've been swimming in this lake longer than you've been alive, 'Boy', so get a fucking grip and stay away from me." His shocked look made her feel a bit vindicated and with that she turned and left him standing there as she continued to make her way to the bow.

The sun felt amazing as it warmed her chilled skin. It also helped to calm her temper a bit. She rolled over onto her stomach once her front felt dry and his hands came out of nowhere massaging her back. She felt the cool lotion and realized he was putting sunscreen on her. She turned her head to look at him and he was smirking at her.

She hadn't totally forgiven him for his massive overreaction to her swim but thanked him.

He smiled that ice-melting smile that she loved as he handed her the lotion.

At that moment it dawned on her that he was in his swim trunks.

He laid down on the chaise next to hers and she covered his back, arms and legs with sunscreen.

She took her spot back and he took her hand in his as they both enjoyed the heat of the day.

She was almost asleep when he pulled her off the lounge. She stretched her arms and looked to see what he was up to. He reached over, retook her hand and was leading her towards the stern of the boat. Another swim she thought.

He handed her a lifejacket and donned his and continued to descend onto the lowest back deck where one of the jet skis was out in the water.

He pushed her in the lake.

Still cold, damn!

He followed and she took great satisfaction with his sudden gasp as the cold water hit him by surprise. He quickly made his way to the jet ski and climbed aboard, beckoning for her to join him.

He reached his hand down to help her up and with an evil grin she pulled him back into the lake and made her way onto the jet ski before he recovered.

"Paybacks are a bitch, Becca... you just wait." But he was smiling so she knew he was having fun. Besides, he started it.

He brought the machine to life and told her to hang on tight and they were off like a flash. She'd never spent any time on one and she was having a ball. They are faster than she'd realized and when he took her over another boat's wake, they got a bit of air. Exhilarating is the only word to explain it.

Once back to the yacht he pulled up to the swim step so neither of them had to get into the lake again. The kid was waiting to grab the rope. He smiled at them both and told them Joel had an early supper ready. With nods and a thank you they headed up to the main deck to find Joel setting food on two placemats.

"You both got some color I see. Please let me know if you need anything else." And with that he left them to eat in private.

Joel's statement was quite accurate.

She realized as did Cain that they put sunscreen on each other's backs but missed their fronts... oops.

Becca pulled her suit down to reveal a rather good burn.

Wherever the life jacket or suit wasn't was now a lovely shade of crimson. Cain wasn't quite as bad but he was very pink.

"Shit, I'm sorry, baby... do you want some aloe lotion before or after dinner?" She wanted it then and there but instead he took her back to their room.

He had the lotion and told her to remove her suit. She reached for the bottle but he shook his head telling her he had this and to strip.

She didn't argue and the depth of her burn was made more apparent. The lotion felt amazing and it didn't sting as much as she thought it would.

Afterwards he handed her a robe to put on.

He also handed her the bottle so she could sooth his pink skin and after, put on a white button-down shirt with a pair of khaki shorts but left the shirt open so his skin could breath.

During dinner they discussed plans for the rest of the evening and the next day since they both knew sex was off the table. *Reality being she had had more sex in the last thirty-six hours than in the last thirty-six years.* She was actually fine just spending time with this incredible man. A man she was getting very attached to. Despite his overreaction to swimming near his boat.

They decided a movie would be good, an early night and more lotion.

The next morning Cain was tan and looking better than ever... she now hated his very existence.

She was sore from her burn and her lips were even swollen.

Her skin was hot and she needed relief, so while he was in the bathroom she slipped out and headed for the back deck two floors down.

The lake would take the heat out. Not her first rodeo with a sunburn.

She made the conscious decision to not get off the ladder so 'Fifty' wouldn't have some fit about her going into the water unsupervised.

She loved her lake... she never thought it would hurt her and it took the fire away. Thank goodness.

Safely back on deck she put her robe on and headed up to the main floor.

He met her on the stairs with his stern but sexy look. "Just tell me where you're going next time please." And with that he took her hand noticing the cooler temperature and with an understanding nod, smiled as he led her back up the galley for their morning coffee.

He let her wear shorts but insisted on a long sleeve cotton shirt from his closet and a hat. Of course, before any clothes were discussed there was more lotion applied and what seemed like a half bottle of sunscreen. He did like to be thorough.

She wasn't going to argue; it felt good to be looked after and he didn't give her any grief about her morning dip.

The launch was ready and waiting to take them back to her cabin. She was happy and sad.

He wanted her to pack up all her belongings and stay on the yacht until they departed for Alaska.

She wanted to stay at the cabin one more night... just because, but wasn't sure if he'd be agreeable.

As they approached the dock, she was all smiles and it didn't go unnoticed.

"You know we are ahead of schedule with the testing. Looks like we can get her ready to pull out and moved mid- week. Maybe you and I should stay a night or two here at the cabin and drive to Seattle and meet up with the crew there?" She was beaming at him. And he was only a bit surprised when she launched herself at him giving him a huge kiss, even with sunburnt lips.

Yep, he could read her like a book.

She was organizing the bedroom while he took inventory of the fridge. He would need to steal a few items from the yacht if they were going to stay here, even for two days.

It was on this day he found out she was terrified of spiders which gave him great pleasure at coming to her rescue.

She kissed her hero a little more passionately than she had really intended and he had no issue reciprocating.

When his hand pulled her closer into him, he could feel the heat of her skin and stopped instantly.

Damn!

She was almost aching for more but he didn't want to irritate her burn. So, she did the one thing that would cool her skin again and maybe her libido at the same time.

Without so much as a word or a bathing suit, she walked down to the dock and off the end without even stopping. Her toes felt the lake bottom and she kicked up to the top. She thought she heard him shout something. But at that moment, the water felt so good and she didn't care or listen... she swam past the cabin and down to where they had a small storage shed about two hundred feet down the beach and was turning back when she saw him standing on the dock. When she got closer, she saw he was holding a towel and smirking. At least she wasn't going to get hit in the head with a lifejacket this time around.

"Get your pretty little ass out of the water, woman... we're heading back to the yacht soon." She went under water and swam the length of the dock to the back ladder. She was a very good swimmer. His look when she climbed up to the dock made her laugh.

"So serious, Mr Curtis," she grinned as she took the towel and headed back up to the cabin, feeling quite refreshed and her skin felt nice and cool.

He followed her shaking his head.

He informed her she had ten minutes to get changed or she'd be going back naked. She wasn't quite sure if he was joking.

Again, it's the little things in life that can bring happiness… like aloe gel. She was very glad she found some in her bathroom. After her very quick change and hanging up her wet clothes on the line in the back of the cabin to dry, she joined him at the launch.

Cabin was locked and she'd be able to pick up her now drying clothes in a couple of days. Leaving made her sad but she knew they'd be back.

She wasn't surprised when he handed her the lifejacket. She'd really need to ask what his deal was. She got safety but he was positively obsessed. His look told her to get the jacket on and with a sigh she did.

Cain tossed the rope to the kid and stepped out of the boat, giving his hand to assist Becca.

He never gave her hand back as they headed to the main floor.

Joel was dishing up a lovely late lunch and she was surprised when Cain told him to keep it warm and continued back to their room.

Once they were inside, he locked the door. That was a tell.

He was unbuttoning his shirt when he turned back around. "Becca, you've been pushing my buttons this whole weekend and now it's my turn. Go into your closet and put on one of those new nighties we got Friday." The light smack on her ass got her attention and off she went.

The second closet was a large walk-in and she never realized how big it was. She'd been living out of

107

her bag the last couple of days. But now all her things were hung up or in the drawers off to the right side. She found her bra and panty sets folded and neatly displayed in the first drawer. Even her sandals and tennis shoes were all up on a shoe rack. And she had still never seen the woman who did all this. Lost in her thoughts the second smack on her ass made her jump and become slightly aroused.

He held up the black cotton one that was very sheer and asked if she needed help putting it on or would she prefer to get fucked in the closet?

With a slight shake of her head he left and told her she had thirty seconds.

She was grateful for the burn and the fact that it hid her blush.

Once in the very short see-through, overpriced handkerchief, she emerged and found him waiting right outside the door. He made a twirling motion with his finger and she complied.

"Very nice. Now please go over to the bed and pull the sheets to the bottom."

She bent over, exposing her bare ass to reach as far as she could and another smack came along with a gentle caress... arousing isn't the word.

She managed to get the sheets down with a few more distractions.

It's a very large bed... custom-made as mentioned earlier.

"Other side too, baby."

And he followed again caressing her ass followed by a quick slap.

Damn! Her whole body was on fire and not from the burn.

He opened the bedside drawer and pulled out the vibrator he purchased as well as handcuffs and some other object.

"Hands above your head please." She was nervous but did as she was told. He attached the cuffs around the frame before securing them to her two wrists.

His kiss was quick to her lips. Too quick for her liking. He spent more time getting her nipples to stand at attention. The fire was increasing in its intensity and she was now aching for him.

He turned on the vibrator and slowly ran it down her neck, across her already sensitive breasts, down her stomach and reaching its final destination he inserted it inside her. Her moan fueled him.

"Be still." And his look was stern but very seductive.

She knew her orgasm was close and she wanted him inside her not that plastic thing. She screamed when he inserted the butt plug, not because it hurt but the orgasm hit at the same time and it was stronger than any she'd had but he wasn't done. "Told you I'd get even, baby." And with that he started to change the vibrator settings, intensifying the multitude of aftershocks into her second climax… her whole body was shaking.

Finally, he pulled out all the sex toys and released her from the handcuffs, and without missing a beat, filled her up with his erection. She didn't think she had anything left to give him but her body reacted to his in ways she never knew possible.

Yep, death by orgasm... he was trying to kill her.

It was dark when he woke her. "Come on, baby. I reheated our food and we both need to eat some dinner." He was holding her robe out for her. As she moved, she could feel how sore she was, all over.

Sex could be a workout... at least with Cain it was.

He wrapped his arms around her as she tied the robe, kissing the top of her head.

She turned around to get a proper kiss and he was more than obliging.

Once seated with food in front of her... she realized that she was starving and made short work of the heavenly pasta dish Joel had made. Cain looked shocked that she'd eaten everything on her plate and asked if she'd like more. She declined but he pressed a second time to make sure. He cleaned his plate as well but did go back for seconds.

Out of nowhere his look got serious. "Shit. We forgot to set up your autopay. Remind me first thing in the morning and we'll get that done."

She nodded, not worried. They had a week to get it all arranged.

She was smiling at him... basically enjoying the view. It was one of her favorites but it made him ask what she was thinking about.

Without missing a beat, "Button pushing." And grinned.

She then got up and clearing their plates, taking them into the galley.

He came up and grabbed her, pinning her to the sink and reclaiming her lips. He also untied the robe for better access. She was gasping when he tied it back up and winked.

"Let's go watch a movie and make out." And with that he took her hand and led her up one deck to the entertainment room.

It was now her second favorite room!

MONDAY— Prepping

Cain made short work of setting up her autopay… it was easier than she thought and only one bill would come directly out of her bank account. He set up all the others to be on her Visa card. He explained she would get mileage every month and more than likely a free ticket each year.

She hadn't even thought of that. She'd only signed up for the card when her dad got sick because it did give her two free tickets and she could fly instead of drive on the many trips she had to make while he was in chemotherapy. She usually traveled alone since her ailing husband couldn't handle sitting or walking for any length of time. In fact, she was the only one in her dad's room when he passed. It crushed her… she was, after all, Daddy's little girl. Her mom was devastated that she wasn't there as was her brother. What they forgot was, she was alone too. Her best friend would call every day to check on her and some days she'd just listen to her sob, telling her that is what best friends do. She owed so much to Mary. Still, the thought of losing the strongest man she'd ever known brought tears to her eyes.

Her new strong man wiped her tear away and she told him she was thinking about her dad.

She loved Cain's hugs. They made her feel safe, loved and wanted.

After breakfast Cain had to help get the yacht ready to pull out in just two days' time. Apparently, it was quite the ordeal. Cain had to hire a company that specializes in moving boats his size and it was very expensive and dangerous. He had to buy special insurance just for the move. It would be a tad under four hundred miles and the cost was just over $100,000.

'How rich was Cain?' She thought.

Becca had to ask why he didn't put the yacht in at Lake Washington and save himself all this expense. He looked baffled by her question but honestly told her it was because of the depth and size of her lake. And finished with, "You were one hell of a perk though." Yep, blush.

The whole day was securing everything inside and out so nothing would be damaged in the move. She helped where she could. Mostly she tried to stay out of the crew's way.

She did take that time to email Mary and ask her to extend the mail hold and check on her place. She promised to call in a day or two and fill her in on the upcoming trip to Alaska.

And she finally met the elusive Mrs Abbot who was in fact, NOT orange but was a petite woman with a radiant smile. Her first name was Stella, which of course

113

made Becca think of ' A Streetcar Named Desire' and smile. Mrs Abbot was used to the reference and therefore liked to be called anything else. Becca liked her instantly and as it turned out, she was 'the kid's' mom and married to the captain.

Way to keep it all in the family, Cain.

The last crew member was Frank Evans and she met him by total accident as he was coming from the engine room and scared the crap out of her. Apparently, he helped design the boat with Cain. They'd known each other since college. He went so far as to tell Becca that he'd never seen Cain this happy and patted her shoulder as he continued to the crew quarters. That made both her head and heart happy.

With the kitchen being squared away, Joel put out all the fixings for sandwiches and everyone came off and on to have a bit of lunch. Becca chose an apple and went out on deck since she was feeling a bit useless.

Cain joined her with his two sandwiches, asking her if that was all she chose. She lied.

Her numbers were very good but without any hiking or swimming she felt like she could gain weight and she wasn't having any of that. And before you ask, yes, there was a very nice gym on board but that is something she'd never gotten into. In her mind, gyms were for the trim and fit only. You might as well put a sign out that reads 'chubby and fat' need not enter.

Stupid yes, but she couldn't help the way she felt.

114

He broke her thoughts... "I know you're bored. But this is the only pain in the ass part of the process, I promise." She nodded and gave him a small smile. "How about I take you to the cabin in the morning and you drive around the lake and meet us at the south end where we'll be pulling the boat out on Wednesday morning? Then you and I can go spend a day or two at the cabin before heading to Seattle. The crew is flying and Frank will be taking them to the airport. He wants to follow 'SIRA' all the way to her destination."

She saw something in his eye on the final sentence and it didn't take long for the bells and whistles to go off. "Why don't you go with Frank and make sure your baby is okay on her journey and I'll take the crew to the airport? Then I'll get the cabin in order and drive to Seattle and meet you at the docks?"

You'd have thought she'd given him a million dollars with the look he gave her. "You sure? I don't like the idea of you driving by yourself."

She shook her head. How did he think she got to the cabin in the first place? "I'll be fine. It's like a six and half hour drive. And besides, you need to be there when they put her back into the water. So, it's a plan... you'll take me to the cabin in the morning and I'll come pick up the crew on Wednesday and take them to the airport and meet you in Seattle on Friday."

He shook his head. "I'll take you to the cabin tomorrow but you need to drive back to the yacht and spend the night with me. Then you can take the crew to the airport the next morning and meet me in Seattle on Thursday. I can handle one night away from you, not three."

She agreed.

He was so sweet.

THE CABIN

It felt strange watching Cain driving away. He looked back and waved at Becca who was standing on the dock with her bag in hand.

The cabin which always gave her peace now seemed lonely and almost uninviting.

'Come on, Becs... move your ass.' She had to buck up and get the cabin ready for her brother's stay; he was coming that weekend. She never liked to leave it looking untidy.

She knew she'd need to change the sheets since she and Cain had made quite a mess of them on their one time using the bed. That made her smile.

She thought it might be nice to wash them and the few towels she used before his arrival... being a good sister. Even if he was a bit of a jackass. Or hiding the evidence. Either way.

Her phone buzzed... she'd realized that she'd left it on the charger since they were there Sunday. Wow... that's a first. She never even missed it.

It was Cain. He texted her that he was coming back, which made no sense but it sure brought a huge smile to her face.

She also needed to address the six text messages from Mary... each getting more frantic when she hadn't gotten a response in a timely manner. 'Aw hell.'

First things first, she need to respond to her very best friend and let her know all was well. She did tell a little white lie, saying she'd lost her charger and didn't get back into town for a new one, until that day. She sure as hell wasn't going to tell anyone about Cain... not by text.

Becca had just finished sweeping and mopping the kitchen floor when she heard the launch. The kid was driving and stopped only long enough to drop Cain off on the dock.

Damn, that man looked good.

Up the stairs he came and scooped her into his arms and kissed her like they'd been apart for days instead of maybe two hours.

Heart slowly getting back to normal from his all-consuming kiss, she managed a 'Hi' with a quizzical look.

"It dawned on me as soon as I was halfway back to the boat that you and I could spend the night here and go in the morning to supervise them loading her up. And that way I can help you straighten up the cabin and then we'll follow the boat to Seattle, together."

She loved the idea and told him so.

And if she was being totally honest with herself, she hated driving in Seattle and didn't like the idea of sleeping without him even one night.

She was utterly besotted by this man.

But if he didn't stop kissing her like that, they'd never get any cleaning done.

She was doubly glad she hadn't changed the sheets yet.

SEATTLE

The loading went off without a hitch. 'SIRA' was safely aboard her transport and heading to the port of Seattle.

You could have cut the tension coming off both Cain and Frank with a knife but both gave a huge sigh of relief once she was on the move.

Frank then loaded up all the crew's gear and was heading for Spokane International Airport to drop off the captain, his wife and the kid. Joel decided to ride to Seattle with Frank to keep him company, plus it turns out he doesn't much like to fly.

Becca and Cain would be following the boat the entire way. It was going to be a very slow-moving caravan so they would need to use flashers the entire trip. And of course, he insisted on driving her car but to appease her, she had complete control of the music selection. SCORE!

The drive was indeed boring and not even good music could make it better.

She was lost in thought when he decided to quiz her a bit about her life before. He also wanted her to explain his nickname.

She took the same opportunity to ask him a few questions as well.

He now knew she worked in sales and marketing for over twenty-five years before moving into medical transcription… she had to make the change because it gave her more free time to travel when her dad got sick and then of course her husband. It wasn't exciting by any means and she missed interacting with people but it paid the bills. It was a huge pay cut for her but… 'Life is a sacrifice.'

She had to be much more frugal with her money and her retirement would be delayed to, well never.

She also told him that she had a small monetary inheritance from her folks, but it was the cabin that was worth big bucks. She used the money they left her to take care of insurance and taxes. Her brother and his two sons offered to buy her share if she ever wanted to sell. She didn't. Not yet.

He quizzed her as to what her husband left her, probably to gauge her financial situation. He told her that he didn't like her saying she'd never retire. He was a bit shocked when she told him that her late husband's insurance policy went to his daughters; he had two from his first marriage. The youngest used a portion of hers to buy her dad's truck which was in excellent condition and had low miles. Becca used that money to pay for his cremation and memorial. He already knew that her home in Nevada was paid but it was still tough for her to pay all the bills without working mostly full-time.

He told her that he disliked her late husband more and more. She laughed and welcomed him to the club.

"Baby, why in the hell did you stay?"

She told him the vows said better or worse... and stopped because he wasn't allowed to know how worse it got for her. The sadness in her eyes gave him a clue.

She changed the subject and found out that Cain worked with thirty active clients and another twelve that had retired. It's more work than he'd like but since he used up most of his savings on getting his boat built, he took on a few more clients the last two years. He'd been saving for over twenty years for 'SIRA' so in the end it was all worth it to him. He also told her that he should be able to stash enough cash to semi-retire in ten to twelve years, depending on how much traveling he does. His sweet girl takes a lot of fuel and the crew needs a paycheck too.

So, just a few years older than she is now and he could almost retire, wow. That made her happy for him and a bit depressed since she knew she'd never be in that position. Unless she sold her half of the cabin.

And no, she didn't explain the nickname.

Lunch was fast food which she hated but knew he wanted to keep up with the convoy. He insisted she get something. He shook his head when she ate her burger without its bun.

She fell asleep somewhere around Walla Walla she guessed. He woke her once they made it to Seattle. The sun was on its downward trajectory getting ready to bid goodnight. She apologized for being a bad co-pilot. He laughed and kissed her hand. "I think I kept you up too late last night."

'Lord, give me strength,' she thought. That smile with those lips, damn.

They were parked at the Marriott overlooking Elliott Bay which is part of Puget Sound. The view was amazing with the lights from Seattle shining on the water. She knew it would be stunning once the sun actually set.

Cain had both their bags and took Becca's hand as they walked towards the hotel.

It was quite grand and she felt like a fish out of water but Cain took everything in his stride. As usual.

Their room was very nice with the same view of the Sound and even had a private balcony.

She thought he'd be exhausted and suggested room service but he wanted to take her out to dinner. He chose AQUA, a very nice seafood restaurant near the hotel. They walked to dinner and it felt good stretching her legs after being in the car the better part of the day.

The restaurant was relaxing with a wall of windows. Cain asked if she minded him having a glass of wine. He didn't need her permission and told him that. Besides he deserved a drink after that drive.

She knew why he asked but he'd only had one beer since she met him so she already was aware he didn't drink very often. All three of her other sexual partners drank. In fact, Cain was the first man who was sober when they first fucked and that was huge for her self-doubt.

She smiled because she knew Cain hated her using that word; he could but not her. 'Hypocrite.'

She looked up and he was staring at her... again she apologized for her lack of attention.

He handed her his wine to try, which she did and handed it back. She didn't care for wine. Water or iced tea was just fine for her.

Oysters arrived and she realized just how zoned out she was since she didn't remember him ordering them.

She hated oysters... she thought they tasted like fishy liver. Bad combo.

"Try one. They are good when fresh."

She shook her head and said no thanks. He ate two and grinned. She was glad he was enjoying them, yuck.

And yes, she was well aware of them supposedly being an aphrodisiac. He didn't need any help in that department.

He got up and leaned over her with an oyster in his hand. "One please for me." She let him tip her head back and put the slimy bivalve in her mouth. It was briny and slid down her throat with ease. Still not a fan. He ate the other three.

She did however eat all her shrimp cocktail and a good portion of the Caesar salad with blackened halibut while Cain made quick work of his salmon and the rest of her salad.

On the walk back to the hotel... Cain was walking slower and rubbing his neck and she knew exactly what they were going to do once back to their room.

Gutter minds. No.

She pulled out her lotion and told him he was getting a back massage. He didn't argue in the slightest.

She started on his very tense neck and worked out several knotted areas and moved down to mid back.

His moans told her that he needed this more than anything.

By the time she worked down to his lower back he was sound asleep. She covered him up with the sheets and let him get the rest he needed and deserved.

She wasn't as tired since she had the opportunity to sleep in the car on the trip over so, she decided now was a good time to catch up with her best friend, Mary. Becca hadn't talked to her in several days and emailing and asking her to extend her mail hold and look in on her place once or twice while she was traveling with only two follow up text messages isn't the same as actually talking and she had promised to call with more details.

She went out on the balcony so she wouldn't disturb Cain. The view was quite breathtaking now that the sun had set.

Becca decided to video chat and Mary answered on the first ring. "Where have you been, girlfriend? I was thinking of sending out search parties. You said you'd call and explain all this travel business but then nothing for days."

It's hard to get a word in when she's on a roll, so Becca waited for an opportunity to break into the conversation.

"You look fabulous by the way. Happy. I miss you. So, I got the post office to extend your mail hold for another month only, which they don't like to do but it's a small town. After that I'll just pick it up for you. Everything is fine at your place. I did water your trees since they were looking particularly parched. I can't believe I'm not going to see you for almost two and half months. That sucks, Becs."

Finally, an opening.

"I met someone, Mary, and he is amazing and beautiful and kind and if I'm not careful I may fall madly in love with him. And thanks for doing all that for me and I miss you too." Becca figured that would get her going.

Never fails.

"I'm sorry… you what? When? How? Please tell me you've had sex."

Even her best friend can make her blush.

"Okay, so we met at the cabin just over a week ago actually but it seems so much longer. And yes, we have, many, many times."

She's pretty sure her friend actually squealed. Good woman.

The rest of their chat was normal banter and catching up stuff but it felt good to Becca. She had been missing her friend. She didn't have that many so she treasured the ones she did have.

By the time they said their goodnights and I love you's, Becca was yawning and ready to get some much-needed sleep.

She was careful not to bother Cain when she climbed into bed. It was a king size bed so she was pretty safe.

Have you not been paying attention? It's like he senses her presence.

His arms reached over and pulled her to him.

He kissed her and thanked her for the wonderful backrub and sleep took them both.

LAUNCH DAY

She was chilled when she woke and there were no arms to keep her warm. With a quick check she could see Cain was fully dressed, and on the balcony, looking very unhappy as he spoke with someone on his phone. The door slightly ajar was the cool ocean breeze she'd felt.

No time like the present to get up and head into the bathroom.

She'd forgotten she wore the pink baby doll with very exposed sides to bed and turned when she heard him rap on the glass door. She turned as he mouthed for her to get back in bed. She would have, but other things were far more pressing at the time so with a small shake of her head she continued to her destination, locking the door behind her.

This called for privacy.

She always thought it was funny that writers never talked about relationships and bodily functions. It made her laugh since Cain wasn't bashful about much and would warn her to use the guest bathroom on occasion and they both got the giggles one night regarding sex and farts. But with all that, she did like a little privacy when it came to her colon functions.

She was in the shower when she heard the rap on the door. She finished rinsing off hearing two more louder knocks. So 'Fifty', shit.

Wrapped in a towel she opened the door with, "Can I help you?"

"Yes, as a matter of fact you can. Get your ass back in bed please. And why did you lock the door?"

She smiled and gave him a quick kiss and headed to get her clothes. "It's launch day, Cain, and I know you don't want to miss a minute of seeing your girl getting put back into the water. So, how about I wear the pink cloth tonight when I have your full attention?" She could tell he was about to pounce when his phone vibrated. That wicked smile turned to an unsatisfied nod.

Her body cursed the phone. Her head wanted coffee. And her heart was seriously beginning to love this man.

Bells Harbor Marina was in the Port of Seattle and was the place in charge of getting 'SIRA' safely into the bay. It was quite a process and would take some time. Unlike her lake, the ocean had tides, currents and loads of other boat traffic.

The earlier call that seemed to upset Cain was the harbor master letting him know that he was bumped to two p.m. for his launch.

The call that interrupted his morning carnal ideas was Frank talking about long-term parking for both of their SUVs as well as getting Joel and all the new supplies to the yacht along with crew. They would need both vehicles and it still might take two trips.

Cain asked her permission for Joel to drive her car and of course it was fine, but she liked that he asked and didn't assume.

Pike Place Market was just a few blocks away, so Cain suggested walking and grabbing some breakfast.

They walked hand in hand and got a few looks that he didn't notice and she couldn't ignore. It was the first time she asked him why her and not some supermodel. He was rich and handsome enough to have anyone. His answer floored her. "Becca, you make me happy so please stop with the 'I can do better shit'. I find it insulting for the both of us and you should know that." His look was stern and still sexy as hell.

She leaned into his arm and he put it around her as they continued their walk. Fuck the looks, she was with her guy.

After breakfast, Becca and Cain looked around the market and ran into Joel buying fresh seafood and produce. He asked Becca to help pick out some of her favorite fruits and while she was busy, Cain went into one of the bookstores they'd passed. He came out with his purchases just as Becca and Joel were finishing up. He was glad Joel was gay or he may have had to have words when he hugged his girl.

She'd never seen Cain reading a novel so she asked what he purchased. He just smiled and changed the subject to jeans.

Weird transition, she thought.

He took her hand and started the climb up the hill away from the harbor.

If you've ever been to Seattle, you'll understand that they are quite proud of their hills. And it was straight up for several blocks.

It looked like he was taking her back to Macy's, but she had a better idea and led him to the Rack, a discount house for Nordstrom's and much more affordable.

She found two pairs of jeans that fit her and were two sizes smaller which made her happy. Meanwhile, Cain found her two dresses and several sweaters. She didn't need all that, but he really didn't like taking 'no' for an answer and he liked it even less when she tried to pay.

He somewhat jokingly told her, "You know most women would like a guy who wants to spoil them."

She replied, a tad exasperated, "You should really go find one of those."

He smacked her ass a bit hard and shook his head. "Nope, you're stuck with me. Get used to it." And with that, he took the bags in one hand and hers in the other and headed back to the harbor.

And stuck on him she was.

If you ever want to see a nail-biting occurrence, watch a one hundred-foot boat getting launched. It's not like you just back down a ramp and you're through. Nope, it takes a humungous crane or two with a dozen plus guys all working in unison. It can take hours.

Becca noticed Cain wasn't breathing for most of the ordeal but once his baby was safely in the water, he gave her a very tension-relieving kiss, and now it was her turn having trouble catching her breath.

Damn she loved his kisses.

Captain Lawrence and Frank would move 'SIRA' to an outer dock that fit her size better and that's where the crew, supplies as well as Cain and Becca, would board her.

They would be in port for at least one more day getting her ready for the cold ocean waters of Alaska.

Joel and the kid were pushing carts full of supplies towards the outer docks as was Mrs Abbot. Becca took Cain's overnight bag onto her free shoulder and their earlier purchases so he could help with the heavy cart. It really was as big as Stella was.

Cain tried to grab the bags and put them on the already overflowing cart, but Becca was having none of that and walked ahead of him shaking her head. She did however let Mrs Abbot take a bag since she was looking like she needed something to carry. Becca totally related to that.

When she looked back at Cain, he wasn't exactly smiling but he didn't look mad either. Good.

By the time they made their way out to one of the farthest fingers in the marina, the lovely 'SIRA' was waiting for them. Frank and two other men were tying her up with lines that were at least two or three inches thick. She's a brute.

Becca took Cain's bag back from Mrs Abbot and boarded the yacht and headed to their room. She was making quick work of hanging up her new purchases and putting away her bathroom items when he was behind her. He reminded her about her promise earlier in the day regarding sleeping attire and gave her a very passionate reminder. He then told her he needed to help Frank for an hour or two while the rest of the crew got supplies loaded and situated. She asked how she could help and he told her Joel might like some help in the galley. That made her smile. Another kiss and he was gone. Damn that man... coming and going, he was gorgeous.

She finished unpacking Cain's bag and put the book bag on his nightstand without looking at his purchases. She didn't want to invade his privacy, even though she was very curious.

In the galley she found Joel up to his ears in fruit, veggies and dairy. He loved the help and the two of them made short work on getting things stored. Once the canned goods and meat and seafood were taken care of it was starting to get dusk outside.

She knew everyone was going to be tired so she asked Joel what he thought about ordering fish and chips for everyone from Ivar's. She'd been to the popular restaurant a few times and loved it.

Joel thought the idea was brilliant since he was in fact, too damn tired, to cook.

They worked out the order together and she got on her phone with Grubhub to deliver to the top of the main dock. She gave them her credit card number and they would call her when they were ten minutes out.

"Miss Becca, you should have let me pay, I have an expense account for the boat. Mr Cain won't be happy with me." She suggested they not tell him. Besides she wanted to do something for the crew since they were all so very kind to her. Joel begrudgingly agreed with the caveat that he wouldn't lie if asked directly who paid. She nodded.

Cain came up shortly after, smelling of diesel and desperately in need of a shower or two. He stopped long enough to suggest they order out and Joel told him it was already taken care of. With a 'You're a good man, Joel', he was off to take a shower.

Becca's feelings could have been hurt but the truth was she wanted to avoid him being angry at Joel and really, that was more important. She hadn't done it to get thanks but to give them. Anonymous was perfectly fine.

Cain was still in the shower when the call came that the cab would be arriving soon. Becca was getting ready to head out and grab the food when Joel said he'd go. She reminded him that he couldn't sign her name on the credit card so they both went.

She texted Cain she was helping Joel get the food so he didn't wonder where she'd gone. 'Good thinking, Becs.'

With tip and delivery, the bill was just around $225 but she was more than happy to pay it. Joel was still not happy but thanked her for being so thoughtful knowing that he would be the only one who would ever know. She really liked Joel.

It took them both to carry the mountain of food back to the boat.

The whole crew ate in the main salon and everyone thanked Joel and Cain for a wonderful dinner. Nothing was left of the fish and chips and chowder, and Becca sat quietly eating her Caesar salad and winked at Joel when no one was looking.

She was brushing her teeth when Cain came in the bathroom with his arms folded like he was miffed. 'What now?' she thought... 'Fuck, he knows about dinner... how?'

"So, you bought dinner and lied to me." She spit out the remaining toothpaste and rinsed before turning to face his accusation.

"Yes, I wanted to thank your amazing crew so I bought dinner. And I didn't lie... I just never corrected your assumption." Which in fact was a bit of a lie.

"You sat there and let the crew thank me and Joel for dinner when they should have thanked you. That's a lie, Becca. You should have told me... did you really think I would have been mad?"

135

"Yes, as a matter of fact I did. So, I did fib; lie is a bit strong, and for that I am sorry." She went to leave the bathroom only to be stopped by his embrace.

"Well, thank you for dinner and may I please have your credit card receipt so I can reimburse you?"

She shook her head, kissed his cheek and said, "You're welcome," with a big grin.

It was too early for bed so she suggested a movie which he declined and headed out of the stateroom towards his study.

She figured he must still be mad so she decided to take a walk on the docks. Give him space and her a break from the stress she was feeling.

'So much for good deeds going unpunished,' she thought.

There were lots of fingers in the marina with so many boats, it took her over an hour to get from one end to the other after going down each one.

When her phone rang, she nearly jumped out of her skin. Of course, it was Cain and he didn't sound angry just very concerned. "Baby, where are you? It's dark outside and I've looked around this boat twice." She told him she was on the docks taking a walk and was just getting ready to head back. She was halfway back when Cain met her on the docks.

"Please don't leave the boat without telling me. You had me worried." He pulled her into one of his amazing hugs and she apologized into his chest. She also told him that she thought he was still angry with her since he left so abruptly, and a walk always cleared her head and gave her some distance from the very stressful situation.

"I wasn't mad and I don't want you to feel stressed around me, ever. I'm sorry I made you feel that way. I went to put funds into your bank account to cover dinner but thought better of it and went to find you but you were gone."

She reached up and brought his face to hers and with as much love and affection as she had to give, took his lips to hers.

She never got the chance to put any clothes on that night.

ALASKA BOUND

She woke up before Cain the next morning and watched him sleep for a few minutes. She was again feeling blessed.

A knock on the door startled her and woke Cain. He saw her looking at him and smiled.

He responded to the knock with a, "Yes," and then gave her a rather nice good morning kiss.

It was the captain.

Cain told him he'd meet him in the salon in a minute.

He got up and headed into the bathroom. When he emerged freshly showered, she was staring again... "Enjoying the view, sweetheart?"

She smiled and without missing a beat replied, "Oh yes very much," and headed into the bathroom once he ducked into his closet to get dressed.

When she came out after her quick shower, her pink nightie was laying on the bed with her robe. That man.

She opted for her new jeans and sweater but no shoes or socks. And joined the gentlemen in the salon.

Cain faked disappointment as she wished the captain a good morning and stuck her tongue out at Joel who shrugged.

During coffee she learned that they would be leaving sometime late afternoon on the tide.

They had managed to get her cold water ready in a lot less time with Cain helping Frank. Explains his appearance and smell last night, before his shower.

The winds would be picking up some so they may have a rough ride going through the Strait of Juan de Fuca. After that they would be making their way via the Pacific Ocean to Queen Charlotte Sound on their way to Alaska. From what she could glean from their conversation, they would be on the water for two or three days before their first stop in Ketchikan.

She was excited and nervous since she'd never been on the ocean. She'd swam in it, but she'd never been on a cruise or any boat except on her lake.

Cain took her hand to get her attention and let her know that the Coast Guard was coming and would be running a survival drill along with giving them an inspection. She would have to put on a survival suit and they timed it. 'What?'

He was kidding and she hit him but he did want to show her where the suits were and how to get one on, quick. Just a precaution, but one he felt strongly about.

Of course, he did.

It's not that easy to get in of those neoprene straight-jackets but with his help she managed to get it on and fastened. She felt absolutely stupid and Cain started laughing when she tried to get out of the damn thing.

She was plotting revenge when the kid arrived and told him the Coast Guard was now on board.

He left her to greet his guests and the kid helped her out of that damn red suit.

'Becs, what the fuck are you getting yourself into? You adore this man, but this trip is so far outside your comfort zone. Maybe you should cut and run.' She was overthinking again but the survival suit scared her more than she realized. Her lake wouldn't hurt her but according to Cain the ocean might kill her.

She was walking on the main floor past Joel when he asked her if she would like a smoothie and she realized her stomach was in knots so she declined and went to lie down. Yep... Mrs Abbot already had the room made up, but the sleeping attire was still displayed on the now made bed. She threw it on the floor as she walked by for no other reason than she could. She felt that this might be the end of her lovely fantasy.

She then headed to the large leather chair in the corner, wrapped her arms around her legs and contemplated leaving.

There were no tears but every so often her whole body would shake with fear.

She didn't know how long she sat there but it must have been awhile. Cain came in passing the clothes on the floor and went right to her to see if she was all right. She said no and told him how scared she was.

His arms always made her feel safe, but she started shaking as he held her and told her that he didn't realize she would have this reaction.

He took her hand and led her back to the main salon where the two members of the Coast Guard were going over paperwork with the captain. Cain asked them to repeat their findings to Becca if they wouldn't mind. They didn't.

She felt better once hearing that 'SIRA' was a strong boat and shouldn't have any issues on the trip north. They also laid to rest that she would most likely ever need to don a survival suit. The older of the two chastised Cain for making her think she would be tested. But was also told that it's never a bad idea to know where all emergency gear is stored. While they were all chatting, Joel handed Becca a smoothie since he knew she'd not eaten anything all morning.

Cain raised his eyebrow to her and her look dared him to say anything.

He didn't.

With their Coast Guard inspection complete and permission from the harbor master to leave in just two short hours... the crew went to work getting everything ready for a bit of rough water.

Once they were ready to release the lines, Cain, Becca and the whole crew went on deck to watch Captain Lawrence take her out of port.

With her fears in check she was back to being excited about the adventure.

The strait was chopping but she saw the waves more than felt them, but just three hours later the Pacific was a tad rougher and she got seasick. Cain was quick with the Dramamine but not before she threw up her smoothie… she preferred them going down. The two little pills put her right to sleep.

When she woke, she heard Cain barfing in the bathroom… it seemed everyone was having a slight battle with the sea. She got up and headed to the galley for some cold water. The boat was moving but the waves didn't seem to bother her at that moment and she was grateful. She was more grateful for the ice-cold water. She grabbed Cain a bottle and headed back to the stateroom.

He was sitting on the edge of the bed looking a bit green still. As she passed him the bottle, she saw the two little pills in his hand, Dramamine. She wondered why he hadn't taken them before now.

He looked up and thanked her for the water and took his medicine. She got him into bed and rubbed his back until she heard his breathing change. He was asleep.

She finished her water and joined him.

DAY ONE AT SEA

Becca woke with Cain's arm securely around her and she didn't want to move an inch, but her head was throbbing. She knew she'd not kept anything down but water the day before so if her stomach would be agreeable, she knew she needed some food.

She also realized that they both were still in their clothes. That's one strong little pill. She laughed to herself.

He must have been awake since he asked what was funny and she told him. He didn't find it as amusing but smiled.

"I hate to leave these arms, but I need to get something in my system. I have a whopping headache." He let her go and followed her out of bed. He took her hand after she tested her numbers and escorted her to the galley where Joel was already waiting with fresh hot biscuits and some fresh fruit and yogurt. He offered eggs and sausage but both Cain and Becca said no.

Cain did have coffee, but Becca decided on another cold water. Better safe than sorry.

During breakfast they found out that the kid was having a really hard time and still couldn't keep anything on his stomach including water.

Joel was drinking water but didn't want food. Mrs Abbot was eating lightly like Cain and Becca were and apparently the captain and Frank were fine. She sort of hated them for that.

After a well-needed shower and fresh clothes, Becca asked to use Cain's computer while he was up on the bridge looking at charts and permits. He liked to be in the know and she couldn't blame him; this was his yacht and, in the end, everything was his responsibility.

He brought his laptop out to the main living room and got Becca into the search engines she'd asked for.

It didn't take long to find a few ideas to help with seasickness that were more natural.

She then asked Joel's permission to use the galley and he relinquished with a nod and told her he was going to go lie down for a little while.

She suggested he get a bit of fresh air first. It was supposed to help.

Once Joel left, Becca was alone on the main floor and it seemed oddly quiet. She wished she'd grabbed her iPod out of her car.

'Little late, Becs, get to work,' self-chastising once again and as usual it helped.

An hour later she had a batch of ginger cookies baking and a pot of peppermint tea brewing. It took some time to find everything she needed. Both the ginger and peppermint were supposed to help and she could contest that the tea had indeed made her feel ninety percent better.

When Cain returned, the first batch of cookies were cooling on a rack she managed to find after an ardent search.

"Those smell good. May I?" She nodded and poured him a cup of tea.

She went on to tell him the natural remedies she'd found online and the reasoning for her sudden culinary venture.

"Baby, these taste great and truthfully my stomach is feeling better. You are amazing and when you're through I'd like you to join me in our stateroom." With a wink he took his tea and another cookie and left her to take the next batch of cookies out the oven.

He didn't even touch her and she was having an issue getting her heart to slow down. She was really starting to love that man.

Before anything else she wanted to help the others, so she delivered cookies and tea to Joel and to Mrs Abbot. She gave her enough for her son because she didn't want to overstep and disturb him herself.

She went back and cleaned up the galley and headed to the stateroom where she found her beautiful man sound asleep.

Not wanting to wake him she opted to sit in the corner and read. Just finishing her third chapter she looked up to see Cain watching her.

He smiled and patted the bed wanting her to come join him. She thought she should play hard to get at least once. And shook her head.

That primal look was back and it didn't take long for her to realize she was the quarry.

He was up and unbuttoning his shirt on the way over to her. Her body responded in kind... it wanted him, bad.

She tried playing naive to his intentions and asked if he needed a sandwich; he looked hungry. He shook his head and took away her iPad as he pulled her up to his waiting lips. His tongue made short work of getting the reaction he wanted and soon they were both in attack mode.

She'd lost count of the orgasms he'd given her since they met but every single one was special and she told him just that. His look was adoring and he kissed her lips and then whispered that they weren't done, not even close. Damn that man's stamina.

She was laying in Cain's arms enjoying his warmth when Joel knocked and let them know dinner was ready. It was a bit early but they had missed lunch so both of them were starving.

She was looking for her bra when Cain handed her the pink nightgown and robe. He was insatiable. She gave in, dressed and took his hand as they headed to dinner.

Joel made hamburgers with all the fixings and even baked cottage fries. He had put everything in a buffet format so each person could build their own plate. Smart man. He was also feeding the whole crew from the one galley which made sense to Becca since everyone was getting over their motion sickness. Of course she now also wished she had on more clothing. She was very happy to see the kid up and about and Mrs Abbot gave her a hug and thanked her again for the tea and cookies.

Cain kissed her hand and led her over to the food so she'd get a plate. Still being careful, she opted for a plain burger in a lettuce wrap and cold water. He wasn't happy with her and told her to eat more. She called him 'Fifty' and stuck her tongue out at him.

No one else was in earshot of him letting her know she'd be explaining that name and soon.

She ate everything on her plate which somewhat appeased him, but she wasn't surprised when he asked Joel to make a smoothie and leave it in the refrigerator for later.

After dinner she wanted to take a walk on deck but Cain took her hand leading her back to their room. She couldn't help but shake her head at him. But once alone he took a totally new direction and told her that the time in the car when she read the magazine article to him was a cherished memory for him and he wanted her to do that more often.

So, he pulled out the books he purchased the other morning.

"I was thinking you could read them out loud some nights. Hell, it could be every night if you wish. I love your voice and just want us to be close whenever possible. As long as I can hold you all night, we can do whatever you wish. "She reached up and gave him a tender kiss and took the two books from his hand. Robinson Crusoe was an interesting choice and she'd never read it so that was good. The second book got her attention and the reaction he was looking for... it was 'Fifty Shades of Grey' and she tossed it back on the bed and a resounding hell no.

"Becca, you're the one who brought that book up and gave me the nickname you won't explain so yes you will read it to me or tell me exactly why you call me 'Fifty'."

She was doing the internal battle, deciding which would be better.

She knew she could edit as she read and omit some of the sexapades but he'd still get the gist or maybe just give him highlights and not embarrass herself. Decision made, "I'm reading Robinson Crusoe first."

His look was priceless and incredibly amused. She wasn't.

She went into her closet and came out dressed in jeans and shirt with her new jacket on. He looked a bit shocked when she headed for the door. "Where are you going?"

She looked back and told him for a walk on deck.

He joined her.

As promised, that night she read the first two chapters of Daniel Defoe's classic adventure while cradled in Cain's arms. It was intimate and lovely, and she knew that he now owned her heart.

DAY TWO AT SEA

She woke up alone but he left her a sweet note letting her know he had to get some work done and that he would join her for breakfast. And thanked her for reading to him and was looking forward to that evening's chapters. He signed it with a large 'C'.

She wished he put 'yours' or 'always' but still it was a sweet note.

Maybe she was the only one getting carried away with emotions. Or maybe she should stop overthinking and with that, she got up to take a shower and get ready for the day.

She tested her numbers and wrote it down in her ledger. Not bad and much better than yesterday. Still, without swimming and hiking, she didn't want to eat too much.

She was happy the coffee smelled and tasted amazing. Joel was looking quite a bit healthier too and offered to make her whatever she wanted for breakfast. She said she was waiting for Cain but was told he ate earlier.

So much for his note.

She opted for a yogurt and a second cup of coffee.

Joel knew better than to fuss at her.

Cain would if he found out and that was enough testosterone for her to deal with.

After she ate, she went to grab her jacket; she wanted to make a few laps on the upper deck. Fresh air and some sort of exercise. And no, she still hadn't explored the gym and all its equipment. Not her thing.

Cain was coming out of the bathroom when she entered their room. He shut the door and gave her a little shake to let her know not to go in there. She smiled… he was very thoughtful.

He also apologized that he couldn't join her earlier and said he had two clients that were having issues with the market's fluctuations. His exact words were 'nervous Nellie's'. That made Becca laugh and he was forgiven.

She grabbed her jacket and Cain wanted to know where she was off to and then asked her to wait until he could join her. He didn't like her on deck alone. And then told her the gym had a nice treadmill if she wanted a more challenging walk.

With a quick kiss he was back into his study and Becca headed to the deck to walk around. She valued his opinion but dismissed it since it was stupid.

On lap ten she was feeling the cold. The sun was out but the wind coming off the ocean was nippy.

A hot cup of tea would be nice and just as she was heading to the stairway, she spotted her first whale. "Oh my God, it's a whale!" but no one was there to hear her.

She went to the rail and watched this beautiful creature for as long as it showed itself.

It was a humpback and it was huge. Every bit the size of a bus. *You really need to see them in person to understand their size.* She thought it might be a male since females this time of year should have calves with them. 'Discovery Channel'. It breached only once but it was a sight to behold and she so wished she had a camera.

Okay, now she was freezing.

Back on the main deck she asked Joel if she could get a hot tea. She was trembling a bit when he handed her the mug. He looked concerned and she told him she saw a whale. He was jealous and told her to share next time and gave her a wink as he got back to prepping for lunch.

Cain came out for a coffee refill and joined Becca on the couch and was surprised how cold her lips were when he gave her a kiss.

He raised his eyebrow in disapproval and she told him about the whale.

"I'm happy you saw your first whale, baby, but what exactly were you doing on deck to begin with? Never mind, I know. Why do you insist on defying me?" His look was stern but there was more.

Right out of the pages of a book.

She took another drink of the hot beverage since it was warming her up and like someone turned on a halogen light, she was almost blinded by the realization... 'He's reading that damn book.'

Again, without really talking to anyone but still out loud, "Well, fuck me, I should have called you twitchy." Timing is everything and Cain sprayed coffee on himself and her that time and Joel ended up with a huge case of the giggles.

He took her hand and escorted her back to their room. He told her she might want to get undressed before they got in the shower but either way he didn't care. He undressed quickly and didn't like her slower speed so he assisted in removing the rest of her attire before leading her into the bathroom and into a nice hot shower.

It felt good and warmed her cold skin.

He didn't even let her dry off before he pulled her to the bed and discarded the sheet and blanket on the floor. He pulled out the handcuffs and a jar of cream, she thought. After he secured her to the headboard, he told her not to move or she would find out just how twitchy his palm could get.

His tongue took ownership of her mouth before moving down to her breasts. Once both nipples were standing at full attention he moved down and found her quite wet. His tongue began teasing her clitoris as he inserted two fingers inside her... she moved and got a stern shake of his head.

She was going out of her mind and he was relentless.

She saw him open the jar and stick his finger into the goo and went back to attacking her with fingers and tongue and then she felt him insert his finger into her anus and using the same rhythm of the other two she climaxed and he kept going until she thought she might explode and she did with another powerful orgasm. His look was smug as he pulled out his fingers and replaced them with his very ready erection.

She could feel his release and hers was seconds later and she was beyond spent.

But he wasn't done... how could he not be done.

He brought out the Ben-Wa balls he purchased and rolled them in the goo (KY gel) and inserted them in her and removed the handcuffs. He rolled her over and began massaging her ass. First lightly so she'd feel the balls move. They felt weird. He rolled her over and moving her legs and stroking her inner thighs... well that was stimulating and ended up being a sexual experience she'd never had before, and quite frankly, she wasn't sure she liked. But her body did; it wanted him and she begged him to please give her the release she was craving. He removed the balls and finished what they had started exhausting them both.

She felt the covers coming over her as she and her body were welcoming sleep. Cain's arms came around her and they both succumbed to peaceful slumber.

He was giving her very soft kisses trying to wake her but she just wanted to sleep. She was so tired and it was his fault.

She would need to remember to thank him one day if she lived through today.

He sat her up and put a straw in her mouth. She sucked in the very cold banana smoothie and finished the whole thing. "Thank you, baby. Sleep."

When she finally managed to wake up, she knew that damn book was giving his already voracious sexual appetite even more ideas and now apparently, he understood his former nickname. She needed to find the book and throw it overboard before it killed her. She was beyond fucked and her body was sore in all new ways plus she had a cut on her wrist. Handcuffs are now a hard limit. And those Ben-Wa balls may have to go as well. He made her feel out of control already and those things escalated that to a whole new level. Yep, they had to go.

Cain was asleep next to her and he looked so peaceful… a wicked thought came to her… also out of the book.

She scooted down to where her intended target was and without overthinking she kissed his penis and stroked it until it came to life. She wrapped her mouth around the now erect appendage and slowly started to suck. His moans fueled her assault, but he woke with a start and stopped her. He pulled her to his mouth and gave her a tender kiss and told her 'NO' and to go back to sleep.

She waited for him to fall back to sleep before she got up and went into her closet to dress. She headed up to the entertainment room and sat in the dark wondering when they'd get to Ketchikan. She needed to fly home. She was totally embarrassed and mortified by his rejection and now knew she really must be horrible at oral sex. How could she ever face him again? Maybe she should move into one of the spare guest rooms. She shed a few tears but finally fell asleep in the recliner feeling completely crushed.

DAY THREE AT SEA

The lights came on abruptly and she blinked seeing Cain looking almost afraid. "Oh, thank god. Baby, why are you up here? You scared me to death when I couldn't find you." She just shrugged as she tried to make her way past him. She couldn't even fake a smile. And he'd seen her cry enough. All she wanted to do was crawl into a hole until she could pack and leave.

His arms pulled her back into the TV lounge and he sat her on his lap with her head on his shoulder. "Let's get one thing straight, woman. What you were doing last night felt amazing and one of these days I'll let you finish but my happiness is watching you climax. So, I wasn't telling you 'no' because you did something wrong… it was perfect actually and I adore you for it but next time I'd like to be conscious for the whole event if you don't mind." He felt her tears.

Cain wouldn't let her go until she was talking to him. She was in awe of him knowing exactly what was bothering her and she thanked him for explaining his rejection. He corrected her and said it was more of a delay. She finally looked him the eye and gave him a quick good morning kiss. His words made sense to her head but they still hadn't made it to her heart yet.

"Becca, do not ever leave our bed again when you're upset. Just wake my ass up and talk to me. You know I have a 'twitchy palm' after all." That smile and that fucking book. What a dangerous combination. She was so regretting her nickname choice.

She asked if he'd give her the book now that he was aware of how his former nickname came to be. He agreed as long as she realized he was going to use the 'twitchy' line whenever she made it necessary... like only eating a yogurt for breakfast.

'Damn Joel.' She hated being watched, by everyone it would seem.

She confirmed with a nod.

He released her from his embrace and took her hand and led her down for coffee and a full breakfast. He even insisted she eat the damn toast.

After they ate, Cain excused himself and told her he'd be back in a minute. When he returned, he handed her the book as promised.

She thanked him and excused herself for her own moment. He couldn't help but follow her. She walked up the stairs and went out onto the back deck and before he could stop her, she hurled the book off the boat into the awaiting sea.

His astonished look was nothing compared to her victorious smile. She gave him a quick peck on the cheek and walked towards the gym.

If he insisted she eat that much food, she was going to have to burn some serious calories.

157

Cain came in and went over all the equipment and gave her a few suggestions, but asked her not to use the free weights without a spotter. And then offered to work off breakfast himself if she'd like.

She informed him that he had way too much fun with her yesterday and she and lady parts needed time to recover.

He reminded her that she said, 'Fuck me' and he was just granting her wish.

That wicked smile.

His parting kiss left her weak in the knees... damn that man.

She managed over thirty minutes on the treadmill at a pretty decent incline since she was sweating out of her clothes and according to the display, she did burn off most of her earlier meal.

Mission accomplished and now she wanted a shower.

There was one next to the gym but she'd feel more comfortable in her room so she headed back down to the main floor.

Passing Joel in the galley she asked for a cold bottle of water before continuing her journey.

When she opened the door, Cain was sitting on the edge of the bed looking at her ledger where she logged her fasting numbers each morning.

She had agreed he could look anytime he wanted to alleviate him asking every day which she really hated.

He put it back in her nightstand and gave her a kiss. "After your shower would you come into my study please?" And with that he was out the door.

She headed into the shower wondering what she'd done to be called into the principal's office. She had to laugh at herself.

Freshly cleaned up with her favorite perfume and wearing one of the dresses Cain had picked out for her, she knocked and opened the study door. Cain was on his phone but waved her in. His eyebrow went up when he saw her attire and on a piece of paper wrote down, 'you look and smell good enough to eat.' She smiled and blushed and made a loop around his office to see everything.

He had a nice leather couch on the port side as well as two very sturdy chairs that faced his rather large desk. Three enormous bookshelves were taking up the wall opposite the couch. A few books were strategically placed but it was mostly filled with knick-knacks that she was sure got dusted frequently by Mrs Abbot. The office was spotless.

When his call finished, he came around the desk to take a much closer look at her dress.

"Oh baby, I am a fan of you in a dress. But let's get the panties off since I'll be wanting full access." And with that statement he reached up and removed them.

They proceeded to christen his couch… twice.

So much for recovery time.

When Joel called them to lunch, he refused to give her underwear back.

She was heading to the stateroom to change when he put his arm around her waist and led her towards the dining room. He patted her ass just out of Joel's view and she was blushing when he put their soup and salad on the table.

She managed a thank you and glared at Cain for his boldness.

Joel left to go and feed the crew and as soon as they were alone, he whispered for her to spread her legs. As soon as she did, she felt his fingers; he found her ready and waiting.

Damn that man!

She settled for an orgasm for lunch.

He pulled out his fingers and told her she should eat. She was going to need all her strength.

Oh my.

Once back in his office he had her bent over his desk in minutes and other piece of furniture was christened. His office took over second place on her list of favorite rooms on the yacht.

"Baby, that's all I got. We'll need to pick this up later this evening or tomorrow." He was finally tired she thought. 'About fucking time,' no pun intended.

But just to have some fun as he sat in his chair with her cradled in his arms… she called him a slacker. Her smile made it clear she was teasing but he never backed down from a challenge.

Shaking his head, he had her up on her feet and across the hall into their room in seconds.

He pushed her on the bed and headed into the bathroom. She heard the waterfall faucet come on… the jetted tub. Hell NO!

He really needs to learn to take a joke and she knew she had to leave and find a place to hide even without her panties… shit.

Becca decided on being a fugitive on the bridge since she'd never spent anytime up there and wondered where they were and how this beast of a boat operated. Actually, she just wanted to stay clear of Cain for the next hour or two.

Captain Larry was a very nice man and went over the operating equipment like she was twelve. That was a good thing since it still went over her head. She got the steering part and knots equal miles per hour but other than that he could have been talking Greek.

He did show her the chart that showed they were currently in the Hecate Strait with Graham Island on their port side and British Columbia on their starboard side. And she found that majorly cool.

He also told her that they would be in Alaskan waters sometime in the late evening or early morning and should be able to make Ketchikan by noon depending on cruise ship traffic and a squall that was building up in the Dixon Entrance. He showed her on the chart where it was and then pointed out the storm on the radar. His job was perfectly safe with her around.

She asked if she could just sit and watch for a little while, but he didn't have a chance to answer... Cain found her.

"So, this is where you disappeared to?" and held out his hand for her to take.

She couldn't refuse in front of the captain, so she took his hand as he led her off the bridge. She thanked Larry for the tutorial and wished him a pleasant afternoon.

Once on the stairs she asked Cain if he wanted to watch a movie. He didn't answer but pushed her back into the railing as he claimed her mouth.

So, that would be a no.

Once he let her up for air and a chance to steady her pulse he smiled.

"So, you didn't want a bath?" She shook her head. "Okay, but now you're in trouble for making me search for you... again. What do you think I should do about that?" His hand was caressing her bare ass and they were very exposed on the stairs. But it felt so good she whispered, "Spank me."

"Yes, baby, that is exactly what I'm going to do." They made it to the first guest room and christened another bed on the yacht.

She woke remembering every sexual smack and was glad it was all him and not the tub. She would have told him but he was no longer there and either were any of her clothes. 'Really, Cain.'

He left her a note. 'I just wanted to be sure you'd stay where I left you,' and he signed it Yours, 'Twitchy'.

Yep, still really regretting her choice of nicknames.

He really had a wicked sense of humor and she contemplated whether to just settle in for a long nap, which she could use or to find some sort of cover-up and beat him at his own game.

Who was she kidding? She'd never win as long as her body craved his.

The knock on the door made her heart skip. 'Fuck, Becs, get a grip.' She asked who it was and it was Joel. Cain sent him with a smoothie for her. Of course he did.

She took the sheet off the bed and made a toga and opened the door a crack to take the cold drink. Joel was trying not to laugh. She shut and locked the door and poured the drink down the sink.

She washed it out and realized she didn't thank Joel; she would when she returned the glass. Not his fault.

Her anger should be at Cain and him alone.

She searched every cupboard and drawer and finally found a bathrobe.

Thank goodness they picked the one guest room with the en suite. She took a nice hot shower and washed her hair before realizing there were only hand towels. Great. She dried herself the best she could but left her hair dripping wet, donning the robe and heading to find some clothes.

She put the cleaned glass on the counter as she passed Joel and thanked him. The study door was shut so Cain must be working and once back in their room, she locked the main door and headed into her closet. She dug out her old boy short underwear and a pair of old jeans that needed a belt and her comfy old bra and favorite cold shoulder shirt. She finished her ensemble with socks and tennis shoes. Frumpy maybe but comfy as hell.

There was a rap on the door which she was tempted to ignore but went and let Cain in. He had a smirk on his face, but it changed when he saw her outfit and still dripping wet hair.

He walked past her and into the bathroom and brought out a towel and proceeded to dry her hair. He also apologized, letting her know the smoothie was his first peace offering. And that he was coming in to get her clothes when he found the door locked. He pulled her onto his lap as he sat on the edge of the bed and asked how he could make it up to her.

Her response was quick. "Throw away the handcuffs and Ben-Wa balls."

He agreed without hesitation. She also took the opportunity to let him know that her favorite sex toy was him. And if they only had sex once a week, she would still count herself incredibly lucky.

"Becca, that has to be the nicest thing anyone has ever said to me. But I can do better than once a week. Maybe slow down a bit, unless of course you wear that dress again." She blushed and gave him a very tender kiss. He returned it with a bit more fervor.

"And, baby," pulling at her shirt, "it doesn't matter what you wear. I'm always going to find you attractive and want you out of them." He always knew what to say. She laid her head on his shoulder.

The knock startled them both. It was Joel, and Cain told him to come in but wouldn't let Becca off his lap.

She smiled as Joel came in with two smoothies on a tray. The bright green one was handed to Cain who looked at it dubiously and the much smaller purplish one was hers.

Joel explained, "Dinner is still a couple hours away so think of these as appetizers with extra nutrients." And with that morsel of information he left them with their drinks.

Becca laughed at Cain's expression regarding his drink but it must have tasted good since he finished it rather quickly and nodded for her to do the same. She did as she was told.

But she thought, 'I must remember to thank Joel for the smaller glass.'

After dinner they retired early and Becca read two more chapters of Robinson Crusoe while nestled in Cain's arms.

They both enjoyed a good night's rest.

One they both needed.

ALASKA

They woke up in Alaska waters and everyone was looking forward to reaching their first port and spending some time on terra firma.

At this point I should explain that 'SIRA' being a nice yacht at just over one hundred feet doesn't come close to the real monsters on the water; the cruise ships which are ten times her size. Remember that.

After breakfast they all headed out to the observation deck to look at their new surroundings, including some stunning snowcapped mountains in the distance.

The sun was up but the temperature had a chill and the ocean was a bit active so Becca decided to go and workout in the gym since they had a couple of hours before they would arrive in Ketchikan.

Cain gave her a quick kiss and told her to have fun before he headed to his office and the rest of the crew went about their duties.

Becca had just put in a good forty minutes on the treadmill making sure the incline was a bit higher for better calorie burning; unfortunately, it was also enough that her legs were feeling a bit like jelly when she stepped down.

Without warning the massive yacht took at hard list to port and she was thrown sideways. Her fall was stopped abruptly when her shoulder hit the free weight stand that lined the wall, followed by her head hitting the wall itself.

Headline: Three hundred pounds of free weights against one shoulder...weights win by a landslide. Film at eleven...or not. Strange where the mind goes sometimes.

Becca couldn't move her arm when she tried to stand up and was feeling dizzy. And just a tad concerned since no one was around. She reached up and touched her throbbing head and saw her hand covered in blood when she brought it back down. 'Well shit, that hurt,' was about her only thought since the boat looked fine. It did make her wonder if she'd fainted, not understanding why she lost her balance.

Over the boat's loudspeaker the captain gave his apologies. Apparently, they hit the wake of a passing cruise liner and he didn't have time to change course. He hoped everyone was okay and again apologized.

'Mystery solved,' she thought but now she needed help. She also felt nauseous from her shoulder pain and her head wound was dripping down her neck. She knew they tended to bleed even with the smallest of gashes. Thank goodness blood has never bothered her that much. This seemed a tad worse than she'd ever had before.

She managed to stand… well stagger would be a better description. 'Come on, Becs, you just need to get one floor down and find Cain.' She repeated that five times before she managed to make it down the twelve stairs. Hey at least she didn't fall, giving herself credit for that.

She finally was able to open the door with her good but bloody hand and thought she heard someone yell 'Fuck' before she felt arms around her.

That time she passed out.

She woke on a couch, she thought. She could tell that her arm was wrapped tight against her body and something very cold was on her head. It felt unpleasant but when she reached up to remove it, Cain took her hand and told her 'no' and to lay still.

"I thought you only said that during sex? And by the way, I think I'll go back to not eating; exercise will fuck you up." She heard him chuckling as she welcomed sleep and thought she heard Joel laughing somewhere in the background.

KETCHKIKAN

She heard him calling her but it sounded far away. The second time was closer but she really just wanted to sleep, but on the third call she opened her eyes and saw his worried look.

At that moment she could feel the throbbing from her shoulder but her head seemed to be okay.

She tried to sit up but Cain gently pushed her good shoulder back. "No, baby, you need to stay in bed. We have a doctor coming out to look you over before we move you anymore." That got her attention and her eyes were wide awake. She hated doctors.

She tried to move her hand, arm and shoulder but the wince gave away her pain.

Cain was looking pained himself so that made her more concerned about his well-being and that of the rest of the crew. She hoped no one else got hurt.

She scolded herself, 'You're such bother, Becs. Why did you go and get yourself injured?'

"Is everyone else okay? Are you?" He took her good hand in his.

"Yes, baby, everyone is fine. Frank got a broken finger but you got it the worst." She tried to tell him she was okay but he just shook his head.

She was going to apologize for all the fuss but he beat her to the punch telling her she had nothing to be sorry for. She brought his hand to her lips and kissed it and asked him to please help her into the bathroom.

She was mad he wouldn't leave but did turn around so she could pee in somewhat private. No not at all. She knew he was smirking about her being bashful so she stood without his assistance and got scolded but good. "My legs are fine, Cain. I can walk," was met with him telling her to stop being a pain in the ass and her body had a serious trauma.

She finally asked if she was on the couch earlier and he confirmed she was but he thought she'd be more comfortable in their room so he moved her. Without missing a beat, "Well, I hope you lifted with your legs. Hernias can be a bitch, I hear." He squeezed her hand and gave her his stern look... the one she thought was super sexy. But the knock on the door saved her his lecture.

'Good,' she thought.

The doctor was nice enough until he moved her shoulder and she screamed. Dislocated. A trip to the emergency room was her introduction to Ketchikan.

Good news was she didn't have a concussion, just a really good cut that took five self-absorbing stitches and she was told to limit physical activity for at least a week once they popped her shoulder back into place.

Cain winced more than she did. But they gave her a shot for pain.

It is very hard to watch someone you care about in pain.

She didn't remember the trip back to the boat or how she got back to their stateroom or anything for that matter. Painkillers are an amazing thing.

Becca was so glad they were still in Ketchikan when she woke up the next day. She vaguely remembered being woken up and fed a smoothie and given more pain pills during the evening. Cain wasn't in bed with her but asleep in the leather chair in the corner. He must have stayed up caring for her. Damn she loved him for that. But missed his arms more.

She managed to get up and not disturb him so she could use the bathroom in peace. She jumped when he told her not to lock the door or he'd remove it completely.

'Fucking bat ears,' she smiled to herself.

She must have been taking too long because the next thing she knew he was standing in the door watching her. She started to cry and he came and wrapped her in his arms and asking if she needed pain medication. He laughed when she told him she wanted a shower but didn't know if she was allowed and that was very upsetting to her. She felt gross.

He stripped off his clothes and hers being extra careful when taking her sling off. He then led her into the shower and cautiously washed away the matted blood in her hair and cleaned every inch of her body before wrapping her up in a towel and sitting her on the

171

bed. He put the sling back around her arm and shoulder and carefully towel dried her hair, minding her stitches. He gave her a very nice good morning kiss before heading back into the bathroom.

While he showered, she managed to pull on panties and a pair of sweatpants but there was no way she could get on her bra without his assistance. She hated feeling helpless. She gave a thought to removing the sling for a few minutes but he caught her in her closet. "What the hell, Becca. You don't need clothes on when you're not leaving that bed today."

"The doctor said limited activity… can't we go for a walk around the town? Please. If I get tired, we can come right back." She gave him the most pleading eyes she could and was surprised when he gave in. She'd have to remember how she did that.

She handed him the bra and he told her he was much better at removing them. She smiled…she was well aware.

Captain Larry stopped by during breakfast to apologize again for her getting hurt and she patted his arm telling him she blamed the cruise ship wake, not him and to please not worry about her; she was fine and being well cared for by Cain, who smiled when she said that.

He was even happier when she ate most of her mushroom omelet. "Glad you decided not to boycott food after all." Her look showed confusion and he knew she didn't remember what she said in front of Joel. She was more confused when Joel laughed. It seemed out of context.

Cain was glowering at him but had a smirk so she figured it was between them. And shook it off.

Once finished, Cain took her hand and led her down two flights of stairs and on to the dock. Ketchikan Moorage has a four hundred-foot dock just for the big yachts that come to visit their lovely little hamlet. It was also her first time seeing the airport, which is on an island across from their dock.

You actually have to take a ferry out there to fly away.

She thought that was really cool.

Her excitement was contagious and soon Cain wasn't watching her every step and started to enjoy the day.

She was reading him tidbits about the town during their walk. Tourist guides are a must when getting to know a new place. Plus, this one had a nice map of where the sights were.

Ketchikan is the called the Gateway city since it is the southernmost town as well as the fifth largest in Alaska with just under fourteen thousand residents. One of the locals told them her nickname was 'Rain capital of Alaska' with one hundred and fifty plus inches a year.

Boggles the mind since where Becca calls home gets an average of just under ten inches a year.

They walked the boardwalk through downtown and around one of their three marinas to where Totem Park was located. Ketchikan has the world's largest selection of totem poles and Becca must have gotten pictures of damn near every one.

On their way back to the main hub of town they stopped and grabbed lunch. She found, through her guide, a cute little place that made fish tacos. They both enjoyed it and she got a smile from Cain when she ate every bite of her halibut taco salad, and since they were playing tourist, they both purchased a new polar fleece jacket.

He paid of course but she did offer.

They were heading back to the yacht when the skies opened up and it started to pour. Yep, they were in a temperate rainforest and Ketchikan was living up to her nickname with a vengeance.

They both were drenched and cold by the time they got back to the dock and boarded 'SIRA'. Cain got them both out of their wet clothes and into a very hot shower.

Once warmed up he put her back into a nightgown and back to bed. She kissed him and thanked him for the wonderful and magical day.

That smile… she loved his smile.

"My pleasure, baby. Now please get some rest."

She was totally exhausted and sleep came quick.

OPEN OCEAN

Becca woke with his arms around her. Her favorite way to start any day, although mildly surprised since he was overly careful with regards to her shoulder. The light coming through the windows appeared to be dawn. She slept for over ten hours. She tenderly kissed his chest and he told her it was early and to go back to sleep. She turned to look at the clock but he whispered that it was four a.m. and that they were in the land of the 'Midnight Sun'.

'Right,' she thought. But she really did need to get up.

When she returned, he opened his arms to let her know he wanted her back in bed. She wished it was for more than sleep.

As she snuggled back into his arms, she thanked him for holding her.

"Baby, I always want to hold you. I just need to be a bit gentle with your arm. Besides you called for me twice in your sleep so how could I refuse?" With that loving statement he gave her a very nice kiss. She tried to make it more but her efforts were thwarted. She started to say she could lay still but stopped herself.

She was having an epiphany. Her expression went from reflective to embarrassed in seconds and not realizing she said it out loud, "Well, shit."

Cain's laugh brought her back to the here and now and she wished she could find that proverbial hole to climb into.

"Becca, you are fifty shades of red so I'm guessing you remembered a comment you made two days ago." He was smirking.

She wondered how long he'd been holding on to that reference. Fitting as it was.

"Well, that explains that odd remark about my eating yesterday. And Joel's reaction. So, he heard?"

"Oh yeah and nearly wet himself laughing. You have an amazing wit and it has thrown me on several occasions but that one is the most memorable by far. You definitely lightened a very stressful moment for me." His kiss was more passionate but he stopped before he got carried away. 'Damn!'

An hour later Cain was sleeping soundly and she took that opportunity to take a shower and get out of that stupid sling for a while.

The doctor had given her some exercises but she wasn't supposed to attempt them for forty-eight hours. 'Close enough,' she figured.

She knew better than to lock the door but shut it as quietly as she could.

It felt good to get her arm free of the restraint and she managed to move it above her head with only mild discomfort. But enough that she knew washing her hair was not an option.

She finished undressing and was just turning on the water when his arms wrapped around her.

She told him she could wash herself... his reply was quick and to the point. "I do it better." And with a playful smack on her ass, they showered and dressed for the day.

They were now in open ocean heading to their next stop, the port of Sitka, but it would take just under two full days at sea to get there.

'SIRA' draws too much water so she can't go through the Wrangell Narrows, not even on high tide, so they had to go around which took a bit of time. And if you're wondering... the cruise lines have to go around as well so Captain Larry was taking extra care to avoid any issues with those behemoths.

Every time the captain saw Becca he'd apologize. Another reason she wanted out of that damn contraption. It was just an accident.

Cain had to work for several hours that day and asked her to please read in his study and not go wandering around the boat.

They compromised on her staying in the salon or their room.

She knew, 'Spies would alert him if she strayed.'

Every time she was by herself, she'd remove the sling and do as many exercises as she could handle. Joel busted her twice but didn't say anything.

Cain, on the other hand, was pissed when he caught her and she ended up in his study for the better part of the afternoon.

It wasn't all bad; she did love the view.

That night she read three more chapters of Robinson Crusoe and slept all night in her man's arms. Heaven on earth.

The next morning, she decided it was time she pleasured him and he'd just have to deal. Truth be told she was missing his… prowess.

He was awake but only just and when she started to arouse him, he didn't stop her, instead he stroked her hair, letting her know it felt so very good but she needed to stop before he came. She had other ideas and his release was salty and gave her the satisfaction she needed. "Oh, baby, that was perfection," was music to her ears and she nestled into his arms with her head on his chest. She liked that his heart had an extra beat and it was thanks to her.

When his fingers started to caress her back and moved lower, she informed him she was recuperating.

"You started this so be a good girl and don't move," and his mouth was on hers taking ownership with his very talented tongue.

She did move a lot and took full advantage of her favorite sex toy.

Dry spell over!

That morning he poured them a hot bath and they just enjoyed the relaxing soak. But while he had her full attention, decided to have a rather firm lecture about her lifting and hernia comment. He wanted her to stop any reference to her size or her thinking she was heavier than she was. He told her that she was losing weight if she hadn't noticed and he'd get a scale if she wanted proof. She declined that offer. "I'll be happy to carry you around the boat today if you want proof that I can indeed lift you without much effort." She declined that offer too. "You know I hate it when you're self-deprecating so the next time you have the urge to express self-doubt, I will be putting you over my knee. Please tell me you believe me." She nodded since she knew that look. He gave her a 'lecture over' kiss and massaged her shoulder a bit and helped her with a few exercises.

Her range of motion was getting better so he let her dress herself.

She was deciding what to wear when he walked into her closet. She had bra and panties on; the midnight blue set was her favorite. And she always felt extra sexy wearing them. His look of approval made her proud of her choice. She was holding the second dress he'd picked out in one hand and jeans in the other.

He took the dress, which was a bit longer in the length than the first one she wore but cut deeper in the front which showed more cleavage, and hung it back up in the closet.

He smiled and told her that might not be the best outfit since she was in fact still healing, but when ready he'd be a happy man when she did wear it but reminded her that she wouldn't need a bra or panties when she did.

He then pulled her into his arms and caressed her body. "Baby, why don't you get back in bed and I'll bring you breakfast." His kiss gave her chills and her body was telling him that all she wanted was him.

He removed her panties and bra and carried her to the bed. "Dessert before breakfast. Oh, baby, yes." She never wanted him more than that morning for some reason. It was one of their most passionate escapades and the pleasure he gave her was earth-shattering. She was laying in his arms and found they were both catching their breath.

"Damn, Becca, that was so much more than incredible. I can't find the right word."

She offered up mind-blowing and he nodded.

He got up a bit later and put on his robe before he went to get them both coffees. He told her not to move and she didn't have a problem with that.

He returned with a tray that included coffee for two, a yogurt parfait with berries and two breakfast sandwiches with eggs and sausage.

She chose the coffee and the yogurt. Cain was done with both sandwiches in record time. He had every right to be hungry. When they were done, he got up and moved the tray before climbing back into bed.

Her breasts must have looked lonely because without a lot of warning he decided to give them some serious attention and proceeded in making them quite hard which in turn caused Becca to start to moan and with that enticement his fingers found her more than ready. She was going crazy as he knew she would but he was taking his time before giving her what her body was begging for. She finally pleaded with him. "Please, Cain... I need you. Please make love to me." And that statement brought on the second most passionate experience of the day. She couldn't contain her vocals as she came and his were damn near as loud. They both drifted to sleep quite exhausted.

She was dreaming of him making love to her and woke with him kissing her. "Baby, you were moaning in your sleep. Is your shoulder hurting?" She shook her head and took his lips to hers showing him exactly why she was moaning. His response was immediate. He told her that he liked that she was dreaming of him and he wasn't surprised to find her quite ready for act three of their day in bed.

Joel knocked an hour later with afternoon smoothies but this time Cain wouldn't let him in. He met him at the door and gave him back the morning tray and took the new one. Again, he came back with the bright green smoothie for himself and a smaller one that was pink in color for Becca.

She took the opportunity to make a dash for the bathroom. After finishing her main reason for being in there she took the opportunity to brush her teeth and hair.

Cain was halfway through his shake when she joined him back in bed and took the pink one, which turned out to be strawberry and banana.

She was smirking at him when a thought popped into her mind. One she said out loud. "Well, thank goodness I didn't wear that dress. We might have had sex all day."

He raised up both eyebrows and gave her a wicked grin back.

She then told him act four would and could possibly kill her and perhaps they should get up and look at the calming ocean or paint drying.

He found that amusing but agreed that he was truly spent. And reminded her that they had two acts prior to their bath.

He also followed that up by telling her that making love to her was the best part of the entire trip so far.

She nodded in agreement because she didn't want to cry.

He made her so happy it almost hurt.

Once dressed and the endorphins were calming, she realized her shoulder was aching quite a bit but didn't want to tell Cain.

When she emerged from her closet she was in jeans and a sweater and her sling was back on her arm. She wondered where he kept those painkillers.

Maybe she'd try Tylenol first and avoid asking.

Cain came back into the room. Apparently, he went to give the glasses and second tray back to Joel. He took

182

one look at her face and went into his nightstand and pulled out the bottle of pain meds.

Shaking his head, "You should have told me it was hurting," and with that he took her hand as they went to get her a bottle of water from the galley.

She didn't like him upset at her, especially after such a wonderful day. She told him it didn't hurt until she pulled on the sweater but he didn't care at that point. He handed her a pill and water and stood there while she took it.

He then retrieved her hand and took her to sit in the living room and watch the sky. It was partly cloudy and still bright out. The farther north they went the longer the days were.

He put his arm around her so she could cuddle into his chest.

She was asleep in minutes.

She woke up in bed, propped up with pillows and her arm felt much better. She was also dressed in a camisole and short set. Cain came in with a dinner tray and kept her company while she ate. He wouldn't take the tray away until she finished everything. She did as she was told. And thanked him again for taking such good care of her.

"Always and forever, baby," and gave her a very lovely kiss.

Her heart was leaping but not sexual; just sheer joy at his comment.

Once he returned and changed into his pajama bottoms, he asked if she felt like reading a chapter or two. Of course, she did. She'd do anything for her man. A man whom she was madly in love with.

SITKA

They woke in Sitka, Alaska and Becca felt thoroughly rested. Cain was still out cold so she got up and showered and dressed before he even stirred.

Her shoulder had a twinge of pain but nothing she couldn't handle.

As she emerged from her closet Cain was looking at her like she'd done some sort of misdeed. It wasn't a look he had often so she climbed back on the bed to give him a kiss and he attacked.

"Why are you dressed, woman...? It's more work for me to get you naked and back under these sheets." She faked a pain moan and he let her go with a very concerned look.

Oh, he is going to be so pissed.

She climbed back off the bed, and with a very proud grin said, "Psych. We're in Sitka. Time to go sightseeing. Meet you in the galley for coffee. Oh, and please don't be mad."

She made it to the door before he told her he was in fact quite angry that she used her pain that way and she would pay for her deception later. She totally defused him when she said, "Okay, but Sitka first."

Her excitement was infectious. And he smiled at her as she left.

The one thing she forgot was the sun was up early in Alaska and it was actually only six thirty a.m. and Joel was barely up when she bounded into the salon.

He begged her to not be quite so happy this early as he handed her a cup of coffee.

Cain was taking his time getting ready and she was not going back to hurry him along. He was already a tab miffed at her.

She was eating her yogurt and fruit when he finally joined her.

Damn, he smelled good.

He took the cup of coffee from Joel and kissed Becca's cheek. He also whispered that she was never to pull that stunt again or twitchy would be the least of her problems.

She told him she was sorry.

"Paybacks, Becca, paybacks are coming."

She changed the subject... his threats usually meant something involving sex and that was fine with her.

"So, can we please go the 'Fortress of the Bears' and to the 'Alaska Raptor Center'?"

He finally smiled her favorite smile. "Whatever you want to do, baby, is fine with me." And handed his cup back to get a refill. Joel sat his breakfast plate of biscuits and gravy in front of him, one of his favorites and he smiled. Then asked why she wasn't eating.

She was on a roll that morning for testing his nerves.

"I ate all I'm going to this morning and now I'm going up on deck to look around." And with that she left him staring in disbelief that for the second time in less than an hour she had managed to tick him off.

He found her taking pictures of the town once he finished his meal and calmed himself down.

He knew she was excited so he was trying to shake it off.

When she saw him, she grabbed his arm to show him everything she had taken pictures of and gave him a huge kiss. "This is so utterly amazing. Thank you for bringing me here." And with that statement he wrapped his arms around her.

"How could I not? You are making the trip even more pleasurable for me with your enthusiasm."

"So, I'm forgiven for earlier?"

He held out his hand for her to take and told her, "Hell no. But let's go see some birds and bears."

He could not curb her joy and gave in to the day.

'SIRA' was docked on the transit dock in the main marina of Sitka and it was a bit of a walk to get uptown to grab a cab but along the way she found a tourist magazine and was reading all about their second port of call.

"'Sitka was founded by the Russians in 1799 and is located entirely on Baranof Island and is in fact the largest incorporated city in area in the United States with over forty-eight hundred square miles of which one thousand nine hundred and eleven of those is water. It too is classified as a temperate rainforest with just over one hundred and thirty-one inches each year.

"'Sitka also served as the District of Alaska before the seat of government was moved to Juneau in the early 1900s'."

They walked around town, found a much-needed coffee at a place called 'The Back Door'. After which they got a cab to go see the raptors.

She continued to read to him as they were chauffeured to their destination.

"'The Alaska Raptor Center sits on seventeen acres that borders the Indian River. It was started back in 1980 by two Sitka locals and moved to its current location in 1991.

"'It provides medical treatment for roughly two hundred birds of prey each year. Most are rehabilitated and returned to the wild but some have such severe injuries that they make their home at the center now. There are currently twenty-four birds in permanent residence including bald and golden eagles, falcons, hawks and owls'." He listened and smiled the entire way.

They learned about all the birds' habitats and what caused their injuries during their tour. They also spent over an hour walking around the preserve, taking advantage of the partly sunny skies.

Becca took pictures of everything.

They both were enjoying this time together.

Cain made a rather nice donation as they left which got him a very overzealous kiss from Becca.

Next stop was the 'Fortress of the Bears'. And again, he got read to on the way there.

"'The 'fortress' was started in 2007 to care for rescued bears in a safe and enriching atmosphere. They strive to keep the habitat as natural as possible so there is no exact feeding time. They also tend to hide the food so the bears have to forage. They survive on less than an acre of land so visitors can get within twenty-five feet of these fierce predators. They currently have seven in residence, three black bears and four grizzlies. And survive totally on the generosity of donations and ticket sales'."

Once inside they got roughly a half hour chat about the location and its residents and then they could stay as long as they liked to view the playful bears.

Becca found the whole experience educational and the bears were very entertaining to watch.

After getting about one hundred pictures of the seven bears, Cain asked if she was ready to go and do something else.

He'd been so very sweet to let her do what she wanted all morning it was the least she could do. After saying a sad goodbye to the fortress, she asked what he'd like to do.

He asked the cab driver if he'd give them a tour of the town.

Becca smiled since that is something she wanted to do as well.

They stopped at the Sheldon Jackson Museum to look around, *no relation*, went all around Swan Lake, stopping on occasion for pictures and out to Halibut Point where yes, more pictures were taken and finally over the O'Connell Bridge where the local university and airport were located. It was very much a large town in acreage.

He dropped them back off downtown and directed Cain to the bookstore and directions to a great lunch spot.

During their drive Cain asked if they were almost done with Robinson Crusoe and if so, what would she like to read next.

Becca thought they had maybe four chapters left and suggested in keeping with the classics, 'Treasure Island' or 'Great Expectations'.

Cain agreed and told her they should get both since the trip home would be at least two weeks from the Gulf of Alaska.

She hadn't realized that it would take that long to return home and was doing some mental math in her head when he took her hand to leave the cab. His quizzical look was met with a shrug. That subject would be addressed in a few weeks.

There were several little stores around 'Old Harbor Books' so Cain suggested she go and do some window shopping while he went in to find their reading choices.

She was coming out of Russell's clothing store when he came out with his books. Good timing.

His bag looked like he found more than just two books and she was curious what he'd bought. He told her later and it was time to eat.

He had a point; it was almost two and she was hungry.

They walked to the 'Baranof Fish Market' which was a cute little place and enjoyed a much-needed repast.

Part of her wanted to find something else to do since going back to the boat meant that she'd have to face her earlier faux pas. And he'd had all day to think of a suitable punishment. But she was tired and wouldn't mind laying down for a nap.

Once lunch was all paid for, he reclaimed her hand and headed for the harbor. "Becca, I'm tired so how about we go and relax for a while?"

She nodded.

His extrasensory skills where as usual, spot on.

She woke from her nap to find herself alone in bed and there wasn't even a note. The book bag was on the bed but she thought better of pushing anymore of his buttons that day and left without looking.

She found Cain in the galley chatting with Joel about fishing. No big surprise there. He really wanted to charter a boat and try his hand at landing a halibut.

They both smiled as she approached and she got her usual hello kiss.

Joel asked if she'd like something to drink and she settled on water.

Cain was drinking a beer which he'd done from time to time but this was the first time she'd seen him ask for a second.

He had his third with dinner, Joel's take on fish tacos. They were beyond delicious.

His switch to coffee after dinner made her happy but then he told her she might want to watch a movie or something since he was going to be busy for a short time. And that soured her mood.

He had to work with the captain to get another permit filed to take 'SIRA' into Glacier Bay the next day. Cruise ship traffic would be high so it may take some time before they would get their turn.

He had filed one already but it was for yesterday. He was guessing on arrival dates months ago. The permits are free but still need to be accurate.

The entertainment room was lonely but she still enjoyed watching 'Sherlock Holmes' again and laughed when she found 'The Poseidon Adventure' and 'Titanic' in Cain's DVD collection. 'Weirdo.'

The sun was finally getting lower in the sky but for ten p.m. it was more than light enough to see. 'How does anyone get used to this?' passing thought as she went to find Cain.

The salon was dark since Joel had finished with his duties just after dinner so there was no one there.

She found Cain fast asleep and her heart hurt at the sight.

She pulled the throw off the chair and went back into the living room.

She wrapped herself up and stared out of the windows and watched as the oncoming night sky made its appearance an hour and a half later.

She never shed a tear but the pain was ever present until she had a thought; maybe that was her punishment... he was going to ignore her.

'Well that sucks out loud.'

She finally went to bed just after midnight and didn't even bother to take her clothes off. She slept on top of the sheets with her throw from the chair and taking up as little of the bed as she possibly could.

She woke when he was undressing her. "Baby, we don't do this. I just planned to lie down for a minute and must have crashed. What did I tell you about waking my ass up and not overthinking?" She nodded and told him what her thought was regarding his payback.

"NO! I would never ignore you on purpose. Besides, I have way better plans for my revenge." He stood her up and gave her a nice hug and proceeded to finish removing her clothes and then lifted the sheet for her to get under. He smacked her bare ass and followed her under the sheets and wrapped her up in his arms.

He gave her a goodnight kiss leaving her to wonder, just what was he planning?

GLACIER BAY

Becca woke alone again but he didn't leave her by herself; he left the books he purchased the day before right beside her and each had a sticky note.

The first book, 'Lady Chatterley's Lover' said 'Your punishment begins tonight', the second book 'Fifty Shades of Grey', with a note that read, 'You'll read every word and don't think of throwing it overboard', and the third book, 'Fifty Shades Darker' and it read, 'These three are to be read before we start your reading list.'

Damn that man.

Just the thought of reading him these books was making her wish he was still in bed.

Perfect timing as always, Mr Curtis, he walked in with coffee and before he even had the chance to hand her one, she asked him if she could please have dessert first.

"Why, Ms Jackson, you're recovering from a shoulder injury. I'm not sure that's a good idea." He then put the tray down and took his robe off along with his pajama bottoms and displaced the books as he climbed into bed. "But since I have a sweet tooth, I think we can manage your request," and with that their coffee got ice cold.

Once showered and dressed they went to get hot coffee. Joel took the tray with the untouched coffee and shook his head. Becca swore she heard him say 'rabbits' under his breath but she never mentioned it to anyone, ever.

They were now in Icy Strait and the captain came over the loud speaker to let them know there were whales on the starboard side.

Becca's as well as Joel's faces lit up and they both looked at Cain. He just nodded and they both took off to the upper deck to see them.

There were six humpback whales including one baby and they were having a great time playing it would seem.

At first Becca heard the blowholes followed by seeing the spray. She would see a fluke once in a while. That meant they were diving and they didn't always come right back up. But then two started to breach and slap their fins on the water... it was so incredible.

The 'kid' joined them and was as delighted as she and Joel were.

Later that day, through Google, Becca found out that humpbacks usually don't form long-term bonds and stay together for feeding mostly. She also found out that it's the males that sing. And no one is sure why they breach or slap their fins and flukes on the water. Also, their flukes are like fingerprints... no two are the same.

Cain came up behind her and put her jacket around her and engulfed her in his arms. She leaned back into his chest as they continued to be thoroughly entranced by these majestic creatures.

The show ended way too soon for Becca's liking but she was getting cold even with her coat and Cain's arms. Her shiver was the end of being on deck and she was taken back down to the galley for coffee and a very late breakfast.

Joel thanked Cain for the break and whipped them up a very nice frittata to share.

Once warm and full she headed to their room to grab her meds and brush her teeth. Cain followed with another idea.

NOPE! Not even close.

"Becca baby, what are your thoughts on halibut fishing? I want to charter a trip the day after tomorrow and I need to get a head count of who all wants to join me." Her first thought was 'thank God he asked and didn't assume'. She gave him a small shake and he gave her a quick kiss on the cheek and headed to his office wearing her favorite smile.

'Wait', that gave her an entire day to explore Juneau... the capital city of Alaska alone. She was actually stoked about that thought.

She loved doing everything with Cain but she was also independent, or used to be.

She was sitting at the counter in the galley chatting with Joel when Cain finally came out of his study.

He had his laptop with him and handed it to her telling her that they'd be heading into Glacier Bay and thought she'd like to look at their website.

She did.

While she was in her favorite search engine, she asked him if he found a charter. He had chosen one called 'Best Damn Charters' and had booked the entire day for all five men aboard the yacht.

He also informed her that Mrs Abbot was looking forward to having the boat to herself so she could give it a good clean.

Becca shook her head at that... this boat was spotless as far as she could tell but she didn't have Stella's clean gene either.

Cain took the cup of coffee handed to him and told her that he thought the boat looked just fine as well.

'Kreskin', that should have been his nickname. Damn!

He moved her and the laptop into the living area so she could read him what she found. They'd be in the park in an hour and at that point they would all like to be on deck.

She began her dissertation. "Glacier Bay covers 3.3 million acres and is part of the twenty-five million acre 'World Heritage Site', one of the world's largest protected areas. It's home to over one thousand glaciers with only fifty having names. The longest at forty miles is 'Grand Pacific' and the fastest moving at fifteen feet per day is 'Johns Hopkins'. The park's tallest mountain

197

is 'Mt Fairweather' at over fifteen thousand feet above sea level." Becca showed pictures to Cain as she was telling him about the park.

"It's incredible. You could spend weeks in here and not see it all." Cain was staring at her and she couldn't help but ask why.

"I love your sheer bliss at learning about where we are and where we're going. I love that you're here," and opened his arms for her.

With her head nestled against his chest she told him that she loved that he invited her.

She gave him a kiss and was going to continue her quest for learning but he had better ideas and they ended up making out on the couch until Joel jokingly told them to get a room.

Timing is everything.

The captain announced their start into the bay and Cain told her to go grab her fleece and heavy jacket before going on deck.

She gave him another sweet kiss and asked for a rain check. He just nodded and smiled her favorite smile.

Becca was so glad that the sun was out that day. It was a little chilly but she didn't care, it was breathtaking.

She heard the blows from whales but didn't see them this time, but she did see puffins, sea lions, harbor seals and icebergs.

The captain took them up 'Queen's Inlet' followed by 'Tarr Inlet' and finally up the 'Johns Hopkins Inlet'. It was all so much to take in and she knew she took way too many pictures but she couldn't help herself. When would she ever get this kind of opportunity again and she wanted to remember every second.

She got a few good pictures of Cain that day as well.

The highlight for her and everyone on deck was the calving glacier. The noise it made and the spectacular splash and a baby iceberg was made.

The boat traffic was pretty steady in the park so the captain decided, with Cain's approval, that it was time to make their way to Juneau and settle in for several days.

It was sad to leave such a wondrous place but there was more to see as they continued their journey.

Back inside, Becca headed for their cabin and decided to warm up by taking a hot shower. Cain joined her and redeemed her rain check from earlier.

They reached Juneau just before dinner and the tides were in their favor to make it into Aurora Harbor where they made a reservation since space was limited. In four days' time they'd leave the downtown area and go around Douglas Island and tie up at Auke Bay Harbor where space is more abundant for boats that are 'SIRA' size. They would then start their trek to the interior of the state after another four or five days in the state's capital.

Becca was reading from her iPad, grateful the harbor offered Wi-Fi. "'Juneau proper is nestled at the base of Mount Juneau and Mount Roberts and has been the capital of the state since 1906. Juneau is named for a Quebec gold prospector named 'Joe Juneau' and has just under thirty-two thousand residents. The city unified in 1970 with the city of Douglas and the surrounding Greater Juneau borough to form the current municipality which in area is larger than both Rhode Island and Delaware combined. The Borough covers just over three thousand, two hundred square miles which includes Douglas Island, Thane, the tidal lands, Lemon Creek, what locals call the valley, which includes the Mendenhall Glacier and the vast ice fields behind as well as Auke Bay and to the end of the road. Juneau also is the only capital city other than Honolulu that has no road access to the rest of the state'."

"I'm not boring you, am I?"

He kissed her forehead. "No, baby, never... please continue."

She smiled.

"'Precipitation falls on average two hundred and thirty days per year but the accumulation is just over sixty inches per year. It too is classified as a rainforest. There are thirty glaciers within the ice fields but only Lemon Creek and Mendenhall are visible from Juneau'." She was showing him pictures of the glaciers when Joel called them to dinner.

Later that night after dinner, Cain asked Becca to please finish reading him 'Robinson Crusoe' if she wasn't too tired. She loved reading to him and she liked getting a pass on starting her punishment reading.

He was so quiet she thought he'd fallen asleep. His lips kissed her forehead and he told her again how much he loved her reading to him. She told him she loved him, just not so he could hear.

She slept so peacefully in his arms that night.

JUNEAU

The next morning, she was nestled in the crook of his arm, her favorite place to be and listening to his steady breathing. She didn't want to move for fear of waking him. He seemed to always sense when she was deep in thought and asked her what she was thinking about.

After a minute she asked how he knew she swam every day and hiked when he'd only been on the lake two days when they met.

He was quiet and when she looked up, she was surprised to see Cain blushing.

"You blush... I would never have thought that possible. This must be good... spill!" She was more than intrigued.

He gave her a huge sigh and asked her not to judge him if he told her the whole story.

She nodded.

"Okay, well Frank and I actually came up two weeks before the yacht to give the lake a once over to make sure we could do everything we wanted and to chat with Fish and Game as well as get a couple permits for launching her into the lake." He took another deep breath. "So, one morning we were taking a trip around the whole lake and I spotted your cabin and remarked how much I liked it and then you came out with coffee and headed down to the dock. That morning you were on the phone. With your friend Mary I would guess now." Becca nodded.

"Anyway, you may not realize but your lake is a great eavesdropper and voices carry pretty easily and I got to hear some of your side of the interaction and became quite enamored with you."

Becca was blushing now and couldn't help but ask what he heard.

"It might have been the first time I spit coffee all over myself actually. I couldn't hear every word but you told her 'of course I'm a smart ass, the creator wouldn't be a complete douche and make me frumpy and stupid and besides I quite enjoy entertaining myself at your expense' and whatever she said made you laugh. I was totally infatuated and made the plan then and there to meet you somehow." He kissed her and finished the tale.

"Anyway, I went by your place several times over the following three days and saw you swimming and coming down the hill. So, it was just an educated guess that you did that pretty much every day and I never saw anyone there but you and it made me nervous. You brought all my protective instincts to life. And ten days later we were having our first coffee."

She thought his look was perhaps like a defendant awaiting judgment for some infraction committed. She wasn't sure if she was totally flattered or taken aback that he was her stalker for a short time. Either way, she wasn't going to convey her feelings… not yet.

She reached up and brought his lips to hers and said, "Thank you."

He wanted a tad more clarification.

She just smiled as she got up and headed into the bathroom for a shower.

She wasn't surprised when he joined her. He thought he was better at bathing her anyway… of course that morning he had other ideas and they ended up back in bed.

Where the hell does his stamina come from?

'Who the fuck cares.'

There was a knock on the door so Cain got up, grabbed his robe and went to see who needed his attention.

Apparently, Frank and Joel were off to pick up rental cars and wanted to make sure they got the right size and needed clarification on what length of time should they book them for. This time of year, Juneau is busy with tourism so getting any rental isn't cheap and you get better rates the longer you keep them.

He told them to get an Escalade if that was available or a Navigator and for the second vehicle get anything full size. Book them both for fourteen days to give them time and if they returned them early so be it. He then told them to put themselves on as drivers as well as himself and Becca.

When he climbed back in bed, he told her that after her information regarding Juneau he realized just how spread out it was and figured she'd like wheels to go sightseeing the next day while they were all out fishing. She gave him a very appreciative kiss.

Cain of course took it to a whole new level.

Once they were showered and dressed for real, they realized that their chef was gone, so Becca stepped in and made Cain French toast and bacon for his breakfast. She was very happy to find a smoothie waiting for her in the fridge.

'Good man, Joel.'

Cain finished everything on his plate and while Becca was cleaning up the kitchen, he came around and wrapped his arms around her and thanked her. He also told her that anytime she wanted to cook for him was perfectly fine.

She was beaming from that remark when he went to fetch their jackets.

Becca finished cleaning up the galley to hopefully Joel's standards and was just wiping down the counter when he was back and ready to go.

She took her jacket but said she needed her wallet and he claimed her hand with a small shake. "Just ask and it's yours, baby."

He was frustrating but sweet and she didn't feel like having that argument again for what seemed like the hundredth time.

She had a better idea… she'd look around today and buy it tomorrow when she was alone. Problem solved.

"You buy yourself anything tomorrow that we see today and I'm going to get really 'twitchy' with you." He was smirking at her.

Her look told him he was spot on with his comment and he kissed her hand and chuckled.

At the top of the ramp she found her guide and started looking through the highlights as Cain called for a cab. He told her they could walk back if she would like but he'd heard about the tram and wanted to do that first and get a good feel for the distance.

She found the pages offering more information on their first stop and read him the highlights. "'The Mount Robert's Tramway is owned by the native corporation, Goldbelt. This aerial tram has two gondolas, one named Eagle and the other Raven which represent the Tlingit clans. The tram ascends one thousand eight hundred feet in just six minutes. Once there, the tramway station offers gift shops, viewing stations of Juneau, Douglas Island and Gastineau Channel, a theater and a popular restaurant as well as Lady Baltimore, a rescued eagle that resides on the hill all summer. You'll also find many hiking trails that will take you up and down Mt Roberts which is three thousand, nine hundred and eighteen feet above sea level.'" He was holding her hand and smiling the whole cab ride, which only took about ten minutes.

Before they got out the cab, the driver told them to be sure and swing by the Red Dog for a beer; it's a

Juneau landmark and if they really wanted a treat for lunch, go to Tracy's for some king crab, 'best legs in town'.

Both Becca and Cain thanked him for the information.

There were two huge cruise ships in port when they made their way to the tram and it was packed.

The whole area was. There were several tourist shops, a lot of jewelry stores and a few restaurants. Becca spotted Tracy's and in the other direction they saw a place called 'The Twisted Fish' as well as 'Taku Smokeries'.

Sensory overload for Becca with so many people but Cain was calm and got them in line for tickets. Surprisingly fast considering the amount of people.

Each one of the cars that ascended the side of the mountain could hold sixty people so it didn't take more than half an hour for them to board and be on their way up to the viewing platform.

The young native conductor played a tape telling them about the tram which opened in 1996 but it was the amazing view that struck Becca and she took several photos on the way up.

Cain's arms remained around her the entire time. She wondered if he didn't like heights or if he just liked having her close. Maybe both.

Either way, she didn't ask since she loved being in his arms.

They spent the better part of three hours looking at every view, doing a nature walk and of course meeting the resident bald eagle who was very beautiful and couldn't be set free since someone had shot her with an arrow and blinded one of her eyes.

Cain gave a nice donation and in turn got another appreciative kiss from Becca.

She took her usual abundance of photos and was in awe of the entire facility.

The twenty-minute movie was very informative and enjoyable and neither of them could pronounce any of the native words. Becca would have sat through it again but Cain was ready to move on.

Their last stop before heading back down was to look around the Raven Eagle Gift and Gallery, which featured several local Tlingit artists.

Cain found a silver ring with an eagle and raven head carved into the metal with the birds facing each other. The nice young woman was telling him that those are lovebirds in their culture and he slid it on Becca's finger without any complaint from her whatsoever.

Once out of the store she gave him a hug and thanked him for such an incredible gift.

Her favorite smile never left his face the entire trip down.

She noticed another cruise ship had arrived while they were sightseeing. WOW, they are enormous.

Once back at sea level they made their way to Tracy's King Crab Shack for a late lunch.

It was beyond packed but it came so highly recommended, they waited patiently for their turn.

Cain ordered the Crab Shack Combo with an extra leg. He got a local beer called Alaskan Amber and a bottle of water and the total floored Becca, over $70.00.

She hoped it would be worth it.

It was!

The combo came with crab bisque, crab cakes, garlic rolls and the biggest crab legs either of them had ever seen. Becca managed over half of one leg and tried a bite of the other delicious items and was beyond stuffed. She's still not sure where he put all that food but he managed to finish his full leg and the rest of hers and everything else he ordered.

Before they left, he purchased a 'Best Legs in Town' baseball hat for the fishing trip the next day. She loved how excited he was about his excursion.

After that filling lunch, they decided walking back to the boat was an even better idea. They did a bit of window shopping along the way and stopped and looked in the Red Dog Saloon but Cain was too full for a beer so they bypassed going in but Becca got a nice photo of him coming out the saloon style doors, so very handsome.

Cain did stop by the gift shop and purchased a garter and told her she could model it later.

She shook her head but knew she'd wear it for him.

On the next block they found the 'Alaskan Fudge Company' and stopped to watch them making fresh fudge in the window. It smelled amazing. After consulting her ever handy guild, Becca found out that they had been making their sweet treats for just under forty years.

She never really saw Cain eat sweets but as it turns out, he loved fudge so they made a trip inside. The choices were vast and she thought for a minute he was going to buy one of each flavor they offered, but he opted for only three.

They had great names for their creations as well. Cain chose 'South Franklin Frenzy', 'Glacier Bay Walnut' and 'Taku Toffee'.

South Franklin is the road the Fudge Company is located on, Glacier Bay is self-explanatory and Taku is a glacier that is advancing in Taku inlet, just east of town and also what the locals call the very brisk winds that blow each winter.

Becca was watching them make caramel corn while Cain waited to pay for his guilty pleasure.

Without warning, "What's your favorite chocolate treat?" She at least managed not to scream when he scared the shit out of her.

"I don't eat sugar so it's moot." He took her hand and led her away from the man making fresh caramel in a copper pot to the other side of the store where they had a case of sugar-free candy.

'He's so thoughtful,' and she smiled but told him she didn't need anything.

He's nothing if not persistent.

"One piece. How can I enjoy my fudge if you don't have at least something? Please."

She in fact had a huge sweet tooth and so she made a conscious choice to not eat any.

But since she was planning a hike at the Mendenhall Glacier the next day, maybe one piece might not be too bad.

She chose the white chocolate almond bark because it really was one of her favorites and as usual, he was more than happy to buy her a pound but she told him one piece only would do nicely.

He bought her two.

They continued their trek back to the harbor, passing the Coast Guard station, a museum, a couple of hotels and a local grocery store.

As they rounded the corner, she spotted the twenty-five-foot whale statue near the water's edge by the bridge. It was quite a sight at that distance; as they got closer it was beyond stunning.

"'The one of a kind water feature, was designed by R.T. 'Skip' Wallen as part of the state's fiftieth celebration. The six-and-a-half-ton whale is named 'Tahku' and was completed in 2018'."

The whale sits in a shallow pool and when the water is on it looks like an actual breaching whale.

Becca took a dozen photos or maybe a few more and even Cain was impressed with its grandeur.

They were a tad preoccupied when 'SIRA' arrived in Juneau the night before and missed seeing the whale from the water. She'd make a point of seeing it when they left for Auke Bay in three days.

Cain took her hand and led her away towards the road that would take them the remaining two blocks to the harbor.

She asked if he'd like a nap and his very quick nod made her realize that they both were in need of a rest.

When they got back to the ramp leading down to the docks, Cain pointed to the Lincoln Navigator and a BMW X3 and nodded with approval at the rental choices.

Becca smiled since it really was a guy thing.

Once back aboard the yacht Becca headed to the stateroom since she really needed to pee and she wanted to lie down. Both were accomplished before Cain made it back.

She felt his arm come around her and they both fell asleep.

When Becca awoke, she was alone… she hated that but he did leave her 'Lady Chatterley's Lover' and her garter.

'Well that sucks as a replacement,' was her only thought.

She went and poured herself a hot bath with some honeysuckle and melon bath oils. Very girly combination. No jets required.

His knock startled her and surprised her. He usually just walked in.

She told him it was unlocked and when he saw her in the bath, he faked a very sad face.

Not buying it for a minute she reminded him that he left her alone first.

He made quick work of his clothes and climbed in the tub.

"We had to go and get fishing licenses for tomorrow's trip. I thought I would be back before you woke up." His kiss got her instance forgiveness.

Her soak was even better in his arms but he did mention the oils were not very manly.

She laughed and said Joel might really like that.

He didn't look as amused.

He turned on the jets.

'Damn that man.'

He was heading into the shower looking quite happy with himself. Becca drained the tub and decided she'd had enough water and didn't join him. She grabbed a towel and headed to her closet.

She picked out a pair of sweat pants and her old flannel shirt. She also put the garter on her arm so he could see her wear it.

His wicked grin and head shake told her that's not where it was going to stay.

Joel called dinner and she stuck her tongue out at Cain as she left their room.

Dinner was fresh shrimp from a fisherman just down the dock from them and their amazing chef prepared them three ways.

Becca loved Joel for that.

She wasn't that hungry before but Cain changed all that.

She wouldn't eat without him so Joel got her an ice water with lemon while she waited.

He was there a few minutes later and thanked her for waiting.

Again, it's the little things.

They both enjoyed their shrimp dinner and chatted about the next day's activities.

Cain was truly excited about catching his first halibut and told her the charter had fishing licenses available on board but all the guys wanted to go check out gear at the local Western Auto; again, a guy thing.

"According to the weather forecast, it should be sunny with only a slight breeze." He was smiling.

That made Becca happy as well.

She was wary at the thought of telling him she was planning on hiking up to Nugget Falls. It wasn't that far, less than a mile each way but they had spotted bears in the area according to the website she was perusing earlier.

She opted to tell him she was going to see the glacier and visitors' center and maybe take a drive out the road, just to take more pictures.

"They should have some good hiking trails around the glacier." He was smirking at her.

She nodded. Damn him… busted.

He reached over and undid the first button on her flannel shirt revealing her bare breast underneath. "My, my, Becca, whatever am I going to do with you?"

She quickly buttoned it back and said that he'd done enough with those jets of his. But she purposely omitted any undergarments when she dressed so who was she kidding?

"I love it when you play hard to get." And he undid the button again... his fingers caressed her breast and his lips found hers.

After they'd worked off dinner and how... he handed her the book she was to start reading that night.

She was a tad tired but managed the first chapter which was so incredibly boring to her. Cain fell fast asleep and Becca decided then and there that this book had to go. What some may consider to be early 1900's porn was beyond wordy and she knew she'd never be able to finish it before she jumped overboard at the thought. She also didn't appreciate Shakespeare, again incredibly wordy.

Please don't take offence.

She woke early enjoying the sound of Cain's steady breathing. It wasn't even five yet and the guys had plans to eat and head to the harbor around seven.

She decided he needed a nice send-off for his day of fishing with all the men.

His moans fueled her and his climax gave her great satisfaction for a job well done.

"Baby, I don't think I've ever had that powerful of an orgasm before. Damn, woman." His erratic breathing made her feel very accomplished.

The tap on the door was Joel letting Cain know coffee was ready.

The boys must all be excited about their adventure as well.

He pulled her into a very passionate kiss.

"Baby, you just wait until tonight. I will enjoy thanking you properly." And with that, he was out of bed and in for a shower.

She was in her robe when he headed into his closet to get dressed. She thought about joining him for coffee but thought she'd just let the fishermen have their morning.

When he came out, he held out his hand for her and she told him to go bond with the other men on board and to have a fabulous time.

He gave her another kiss that made her miss him already and reached down and brought her hand with the ring on her finger to his lips and kissed it as well.

"Be careful at the glacier please and the keys to the BMW are on my desk. I'll see you later." She nodded and told him to be safe.

She wanted to say, 'I love you,' but didn't. It just didn't seem like the right time. They'd both sort of skirted the word but never said the three together.

Would they ever?

And did it matter as long as he looked at her with those eyes and that smile?

She headed in for her shower and dressed in jeans, a short sleeve shirt but grabbed her light jacket just in case. She also put on tennis shoes for the hike and put her license and credit card in her back pocket. She needed an ATM for some spending money.

The boys were gone when she went into the salon. She headed to the galley for coffee and Joel left her a note telling her that he had made her a smoothie and she'd find it in the fridge.

That made her smile.

Cain added a PS reminding her to eat lunch which didn't.

'For the love of God, does he think I don't know how to feed myself' right?'...There were a few issues during their first couple of coffees.

With coffee in hand she went to fetch the keys from his desk and found an envelope and another note.

'Thought you might need some spending money,' Yours 'C'.

That made her heart feel really great but the three hundred cash didn't. What in the hell did he think she would need that costs that much?

'Services rendered,' she laughed out loud at that thought.

She took his note, the keys and a twenty-dollar bill and left the remaining cash.

She kept every note he'd ever written her.

Once back in the galley she found a travel mug, transferred the smoothie contents and headed up to the BMW.

Nice car.

She was thrilled it had a built-in GPS and spent a few minutes finding all the things one should before they start driving an unfamiliar car.

When she looked up, Stella was coming up the gangway waving at her.

"Miss Becca, you forgot this and Mr Cain called and asked me to make sure you got your envelope before you left. You have a good time." And with that she handed Becca the envelope with the remaining cash and headed back towards the yacht.

Becca managed a thank you before the petite housekeeper left. Her look must have been total disbelief… how in the hell did he know?

'Cameras?'

Her phone beeped and it was a text from him. 'Thought you might need help remembering your cash. See you later.'

She texted back a thank you and good luck.

It was just easier not to spend his money and avoid a tiff over text.

His final text was short and to the point, 'Twitchy'.

She just shook her head and didn't respond.

She started the car and punched in the destination and headed to the glacier.

'The Mendenhall Glacier did in fact have several good hiking trails. The glacier itself was just under fourteen miles and was over five thousand feet high.' It was also receding at an incredible rate which Becca found exceedingly sad.

She started on the photo trail and thought the name was quite suitable. She did in fact take a dozen or so pictures of the glacier and after a walk around the visitors' center, she took the very leisurely walk up to Nugget Falls, yep, more photos.

Once back in the visitors' center, she found another hiking trail called the East Glacier Trail.

She purchased a water and set out to hike the 3.5-mile loop.

It was much more challenging with its terrain of rocks, gravel and stairs, and took her over two hours to get back to the beginning.

She was exhausted and heading back to the car when she spotted the mama bear and cub.

They seemed to be staring at each other and Becca was a tad scared. Well terrified might be a better word.

The two brown bears were just across the road from her but looked to be advancing her way. Way too close for comfort and then some tourists spotted them as well and being utterly stupid, were trying to get pictures and approaching way too close.

This made Becca realize just how dangerous the situation was getting and she took off running to the rangers' office just up the road to let them know before someone got hurt. They took her name and thanked her.

She got in her car and worked at slowing her heart rate as she caught her breath. Too much adrenaline for one day.

She thought she would omit that last encounter from Cain.

It was well after one and she was starving and no longer interested in driving to the end of the road. She was thinking more of food and a nap.

She'd seen a huge grocery store on the road out to the glacier and decided she'd stop there before heading back to the harbor.

'Fred Meyer' was not just groceries, it had everything, including its own jewelry store. Definitely a one-stop shopping kind of store.

It dawned on her as she picked out an apple that the boys would be tired after their day of fishing and maybe she should fix them all dinner.

A plan formed as she walked around the massive store.

She went and got a cart and headed to the meat department for steaks, back to produce for potatoes, zucchini and mushrooms. Last item was fresh bread from the bakery. Along with her water, apple and KIND bar.

It was good she had all that cash after all. 'Thank you, Cain.'

As she was leaving, she saw the liquor store. Alaska doesn't sell beer or wine in their grocery stores.

On display was 'Summer Ale' from the same local brewery Cain had tried the day before and she thought that would go well with the dinner she planned. She picked up a half rack and headed back to the boat.

She ate both her apple and KIND bar en route. But still had a mild headache.

Parked back at Aurora Harbor she thought about making two trips with her purchases but her shoulder, although much better, didn't like the weight of the beer so she got a cart from the top of the gangway and made one much easier trip down the dock.

Of course, once at the boat it took her a couple of trips to get everything up the two flights of stairs. She didn't want to bother Mrs Abbot, who had been busy… the boat was immaculate.

She got the food and beverages stored and headed to their room for a quick shower and some Tylenol for her head.

It was almost three now so she decided a nap wasn't the best idea and went to prep all the food.

She thought Cain mentioned they'd be back around five or six so that was her timeline for dinner.

It took a while to find all the items needed but it was a very stocked galley and Joel made great use of every inch of it.

She was no chef but could hold her own when it came to such a simple dinner. French bread was covered in butter and garlic and wrapped tight in aluminum foil and ready to be heated on the grill. The zucchini was sliced and marinating in olive oil, garlic and a little bit of cayenne.

Potatoes were cubed and in cold salt water so they wouldn't brown before roasting.

The steaks were 'ribeye's' and didn't need anything but salt and pepper before hitting the grill.

Her dad always told her that a good steak needed simplicity. Never muck it up with sauce.

That thought made her smile.

Everything was ready. She was quite happy with herself.

She went back into their room to retrieve the keys and remaining cash and put them back in Cain's office.

She also took that time alone to draft a very lengthy email to her best friend telling her more about her adventure in Alaska. She attached quite a few pictures, including one of Cain. She thought it was time Mary and he met. Before this day, Becca wanted to keep him all to herself.

She had just hit send on her iPad when her phone lit up like a Christmas tree.

She had nine texts from Cain… they must not have had a signal for part of the day since the times on each were from all throughout the day.

Mostly pictures of fish that made her laugh.

Halibut porn.

The biggest one was apparently caught by the kid and was just over forty pounds and Cain had the next biggest and his grin was bigger than the fish.

The last text said, 'Limited out on halibut and heading for the docks. We're all tired so thinking we'll order something. Hope you had fun and see you soon,' and was sent a half hour ago.

She texted him back, 'Your woman has dinner all in hand for everyone. Get your handsome ass home. Missing you.'

His response was instant, 'Thank you, baby,' followed by several red hearts.

Her own heart loved that.

Time to get dinner going. Potatoes would take over an hour so she needed to get them into the oven. Drained, seasoned and covered in a bit of olive oil... they were ready to get their roast on.

She also took the steaks out and got them seasoned. They needed to be at room temperature before the grill.

She liked watching cooking shows now and then.

It wasn't long before she heard the guys returning but only Cain came up to the main floor.

She went to greet him and he had her to his lips giving her quite the welcome home kiss.

But damn, he needed a shower. She wrinkled her nose.

"I smell, I am aware... be back after my shower unless you'd like to join me." His look wasn't exactly hopeful so she figured he was tired.

She appreciated the offer but told him she'd get dinner finished so they could have an early night.

His smile and nod told her she was spot on.

While all the men were taking their showers, she set the large dining table for seven. She put pitchers of ice water on the table and as each gentleman made his way up to the salon, he was handed a nice cold summer ale.

Truth be told, she didn't like beer but this one had a picture of an orca on it and for that reason only, she bought it.

Happy accident... it got rave reviews from everyone.

The captain even gave his underage son permission to have one.

Good dad!

Joel offered to be grill master so Becca could get the mushrooms and zucchini sautéed. She was wondering how she was going to manage being in two places at once.

She gave him a huge hug since he was as tired as the rest of them.

Dinner was great and full of fishing tales. It was nice to just sit and listen.

The boat that took them out was called the Endeavour, it was a thirty-foot Almar and designed for Alaskan waters. It was manned by Captain Duane who was a local and knew the area very well and had no problem finding them halibut. They moved three times, fishing near Shelter Island, Lincoln Island and Admiralty Island.

She knew the last one since they sailed right by it on their way to Juneau but would have to find the other two on a chart later.

They were also making fun of poor Frank who only caught, 'ping pong paddles', very small halibut that needed to be thrown back so they could grow up.

Poor guy.

They did end up with ten nice fish, the captain guessed about one hundred and fifty to two hundred pounds of meat. The charter took care of getting them cleaned and processed. They would be freezer packed and shipped to wherever Cain wished. But instead, Joel was going to buy a new chest freezer the next day to store their catch onboard.

Once dinner was concluded and everyone thanked Becca for her quick thinking, they all headed to their respective cabins for a much-needed rest.

Cain tried to get her to come with him to bed but Becca wasn't about to leave Joel the huge mess so she went about doing dishes and cleaning up the galley.

When she finished, she found him fast asleep.

After changing into one of her camisole and short sets she joined her man.

She was out cold in seconds.

RAIN!

When she woke, Cain was removing her clothing and making very quick work at getting her in the mood.

Her slight moan was followed up by several more intense ones as he started her day off with a very nice orgasm.

"As promised, baby, thank you for everything you did yesterday." And then made sure that he gave her an extra orgasm or two just to let her know how much he appreciated her. He is nothing if not thorough.

She was nestled in his arms when he asked about her day. "I realized this morning that not once did I ask about your day at the glacier or your drive out to the end of the road. I'm sorry about that."

She wasn't at all upset and told him she very much enjoyed the banter about his trip.

Her hike was more for her anyway.

But she did let him know that she never made it out the road... too tired after her five hours of walking, hiking and running. Leaving out the running part.

"Well it is pouring outside today and I do have to work for a little while. How about you and I take a drive this afternoon?" She nodded with great enthusiasm.

His parting kiss left her breathless as she watched her ever so lovely naked man head into the bathroom.

WOOF!

She fell back to sleep.

She tested low that morning but knew Joel would fix that with one of his protein drinks.

Once dressed for the day she took note of that boring-ass book on her nightstand. She decided then and there that it needed to be destroyed.

She took the book with her when she headed to get coffee.

Joel handed her a cup and made the comment that he loved that book.

Early twentieth-century erotic fiction... of course he does.

She handed him the book with a 'be my guest, it's yours.'

Out of nowhere Cain's very loud voice yelled, "Rebecca Lynne Jackson, get your ass in here, NOW!"

Talking to herself mostly, "Well that can't be good." Joel chuckled but his eyes looked slightly terrified.

Opening his office door and not closing it, "You bellowed?"

Without looking up he read her a story about them closing the 'Sheep Creek' trail at the Mendenhall Glacier yesterday afternoon due to bear activity. Park ranger, Mike Gleason wished to thank visitor Rebecca Lynne

Jackson for alerting them to the very dangerous situation.

'Well fuck!' Again, no good deed goes unpunished.

He looked up and motioned for her to shut the door. She did but after she was on the other side.

She thought, 'The day started off so well.'

She was back having her coffee when he took her hand and asked for her to come with him. His grip was a bit firm and she told him 'no'.

She then told him she saw a mama bear and cub and some tourists were getting way too close and someone could have been hurt. She was never in any danger so she went and told the park.

Little white lie.

"Then why did you purposely omit it from your story this morning?" His look told her he didn't quite believe her account of all the details.

"Because it wasn't the highlight of my day." She pulled her hand free and went to get a refill of coffee since Joel was hiding somewhere. 'Coward.'

He shook his head but gave her a peck on the cheek and went back into his office.

She wasn't sure if all was forgiven but she'd take what she could get.

Joel returned with a sheepish grin and made her a fresh smoothie.

She thanked him and took the smoothie and went up to the gym and walked on the treadmill for half an hour and then using the lightest dumb-bell she could

228

find, worked on getting strength back into her shoulder. After twenty reps she was feeling a twinge and stopped. She used a heavier dumb-bell on her good arm with the same twenty reps, no twinge.

'Don't overdo, Becs.' She was channeling her doctor's orders.

It was still raining and now she wanted off the boat for a little while, still not knowing what mood Cain was in. She dumped the rest of the smoothie down the bathroom sink next to the gym before returning the glass to the galley.

BINGO.

She asked Joel if she could come with him to pick out the new freezer.

He went to get the keys from Cain and to make sure it was okay that Becca went with him.

But he was very busy on the phone and handed Joel the keys motioning for him to leave.

She put a note on his pillow since texting would interrupt his call and he was already displeased with her.

They took the Navigator and it was very comfortable but had a slight fishy smell. She suggested they get some Febreze while they were out. Joel nodded in complete agreement.

He wanted to go to Home Depot and look around first and if need be, they could go to Western Auto or another local supplier.

Who knew buying a freezer would be such an undertaking?

They got lucky and found exactly what he wanted at Home Depot, who would deliver to the harbor the next day.

She found air freshener and it did a nice job making the car smell better.

Joel spotted the Costco just down the hill and stopped to get a few supplies for the coming week. He was very thorough when he shopped and filled the cart nicely.

He also picked up four rotisserie chickens, rolls and potato salad for lunch since they were running a bit late.

Everything paid for and loaded in the car they were heading back to 'SIRA'.

Becca was still glad she tagged along. She liked Joel.

It took two carts, courtesy of the marina, to get everything they bought down the dock. And Joel let her push one. The kid was there waiting to help pack everything inside and Joel refused to let Becca carry anything up the stairs.

She thanked him for the outing and headed up to the salon.

Her head was pounding.

She managed to get only partially wet even though it never stopped raining their entire time out.

Cain was getting a bottle of water and asked if she had fun. She shrugged. He smiled... he knew she didn't like shopping. But it wasn't her smile.

He held his hand for her to take, which she did and he led her back into their room and shut the door. "Becca, please get out of those wet clothes and come into my office when you're done." He gave her another peck on the cheek and headed back to his office.

She now knew she was still in hot water. A peck on the cheek was a good tell. And two in one day… he might as well have been bellowing at her. And he didn't call her baby. 'Well shit!'

She changed into a dry sweater but her jeans were fine, just wet on the bottom of the legs. No reason to give poor Mrs Abbot more laundry. She did however take off the wet shoes and socks.

That's what she needed, new shoes. Wayward thought, but still.

She grabbed her phone to look up shoe stores before facing Cain.

There were several including one called 'Shoefly' right downtown. Perfect.

Joel called everyone to lunch before she had a chance to go face Cain. She wasn't really hungry; stress always made her lose her appetite and her pounding head was making her nauseous.

Cain opened the bedroom door as she was walking towards it and instantly noticed she didn't have on dry jeans. He escorted her back into her closet and pulled a fresh pair off the hanger and asked if she needed help getting them on.

She grabbed them with a bit more force than she intended and the pant leg hit him squarely in the face. His shocked look made her laugh. She apologized when his look became highly miffed. He shook his head and left her alone in her closet.

'Now what? Again, the day started off so good.'

She put on the clean jeans and found she was alone in the stateroom.

She didn't know how to fix 'this' or what the fuck 'this' was exactly.

She knew she didn't want any food but also knew better than to not go out to lunch.

Everyone was already eating when she came out. She felt self-conscious with everyone there. Joel handed her a plate and the thought of eating made her sick to her stomach. Joel instantly noticed that her coloring was off and went to the fridge and got her a smoothie he'd made. Cain took it and said she needed to eat real food.

It was the first time Becca ever heard Joel raise his voice.

"NO, she doesn't. She needs nutrients anyway her body will take them." He took the drink from Cain and handed it back to her.

Becca thanked Joel and left the salon heading for anywhere else. The stress was overwhelming to her. And now she got Joel in trouble.

She made it up one floor and into the spare room with the en suite before she started throwing up

232

violently. By the time Cain found her, she had the dry heaves so bad she'd wet herself.

She was shaking uncontrollably and couldn't even speak. Plus, she was apparently ghost white.

"Becca! Oh shit, baby, stay with me. I'm so sorry. I didn't realize. I didn't mean to stress you out. Come on, stay with me." His voice seemed so far away to her.

He wrapped her up in a blanket and yelled for Frank… "Get the keys now, we have to get to the hospital." His voice was so far away from her and he sounded upset. Almost panicky. 'Why?'

Beeps and buzzing woke her up. She was in a hospital. How the hell did that happen?

She had an IV in her arm and something annoying in her nose, 'oxygen'.

She pulled the nose piece away and sat up looking around. No one was in the room with her. She removed some clapper on her finger and that set off a whole new set of beeps.

It also brought a nurse in to put everything back on and ask Becca how she was feeling.

"Fine thank you, and you?" She was nothing if not courteous.

The nurse was taken aback and said she was fine and left.

Becca was planning her escape when Cain walked in. She instantly started to cry… she hated being a burden and he was so mad at her.

"Baby, what's wrong? Do you hurt?"

"You're mad at me and now I'm back in the fucking hospital, why? You should cut your loses... I suck." He was smirking as he handed her a tissue and kissed her forehead.

"I was annoyed at you, not mad. You hiked yesterday without eating enough and my stressing you out didn't help any. Your numbers didn't just crash, baby. You almost died. I brought you to the hospital in the nick of time and they are currently giving you lots of fluids with electrolytes to regulate your system and get your sugars under control." His expression was pained as he spoke. He continued, "And I consider myself damn lucky to have you in my life. As for your sucking, I believe I enjoyed that the last time, very much"

That brought all her coloring back and then some.

When he gave her an overly passionate kiss... her heart monitor went crazy.

The nurse came back in to check on her.

"Your heart rate is elevated." Becca pointed to Cain.

The nurse shook her head and left the room.

Both of them couldn't help but laugh.

When Cain took her hand, she noticed her ring was gone. Her eyes showed utter panic, thinking she lost it but he pulled it out of his pocket and placed it back on her finger with a kiss.

"Oh, thank goodness. It would break my heart to lose this ring. I treasure it like I treasure you. Now, please get me out of here."

He smiled her smile and told her he felt the same and she'd have to wait for the doctor.

She nodded and fell back asleep.

Her doctor was actually named Dr Jones... nice guy, and he and Cain were chatting about sailing when Becca woke back up.

She interrupted them and asked if she could be set free of the IV. And could Cain take her home please.

The doctor gave her a strict talk about diabetes and told her to stop all medications regarding her disease. She didn't need them and to follow up with her normal GP in a couple months for another A1C. Her current one was too low.

He then asked her a few questions regarding her eating habits and got curious about the day before activities, the one that caused her current situation. "How many miles did you hike yesterday at the glacier?" She told him around six including the East Glacier Trail. "And you drank a smoothie for breakfast, is that all you had?" She nodded telling him she had water and that she also had an apple and KIND bar following the hike. "Did you eat dinner?" She again nodded and Cain filled him in on what little she ate.

"So, you burned over three thousand calories and ate less than one thousand. Do you see the issue?" She nodded.

"And did you eat today?" She shook her head and Cain looked like he was in pain.

She knew he blamed himself. She squeezed his hand with a small 'I'm sorry' smile.

"If you are going to exert energy hiking and exercising you need to increase your food intake by quite a bit." She felt very scolded by Dr Jones and nodded.

The doctor then handed Cain a list of foods to add into her diet and said it would help if he could get her to eat a carbohydrate with breakfast and lunch. And to tell his chef that she needs eighteen hundred to twenty-two hundred calories a day minimum. Spread it over three meals and two snacks each day.

He concluded by telling her that her weight was perfect for her age and height so she needed to stop trying to lose and learn to maintain. "You're lucky your husband got you here when he did." He patted her shoulder and shook Cain's hand. He also signed her discharge papers.

Before the nurse came in to get that damn thing out of her arm, she decided not to ask about the husband's remark but instead, asked him if he was mad at Joel.

He told her he wasn't mad at anyone.

She tried to tell him how sorry she was for all the fuss but he wouldn't let her finish.

"Baby, let's just get you back where you belong. And I can promise you, this is never going to happen again under my watch." His look was stern, but so very sexy.

The nurse came in a few minutes later to release her from her IV bondage. Good, she really had to pee.

Cain handed her a bag with fresh clothes, but no shoes. He carried her to the car and soon they were heading back to the yacht. And yes, he carried her down to the boat as well.

It was still raining.

Becca was under house arrest for the next few days. Cain and Joel monitored everything she ate. She didn't dare complain since she was feeling better and better each day. Despite the incredible amount of food she was forced to consume.

Cain made sure she saw 'Tahku' the whale water feature from the channel when they moved 'SIRA' to Auke Bay.

But she missed being downtown… there was more to look at and more to do. Not that she was allowed to do much.

He let her work out after lunch when he could be there and supervise. He also kept close track of her numbers in the morning and had her testing two hours after lunch and before bed.

She was beginning to feel like a pin cushion.

Their sex life had taken a back seat to her health as well. In fact, she hadn't read to him for the last three nights. She was missing him, even though he was right in front of her working at his desk. She sighed.

He looked up. "What's up, Becca?"

Her first thought was, can we please go have sex but decided on, "Can I please go for a walk? It's not raining and I've been a good patient, haven't I?"

He smiled her smile. "Yes, you have and I think it would be fine for you to go for a walk."

She clapped and was getting ready to leave.

"Baby, don't go crazy... I'd like you back within the hour."

She went around the desk and gave him a kiss goodbye and hurried out the door before he changed his mind.

She heard him chuckling as she shut the door.

Like any newly released prisoner... she had no sense of time as she explored Auke Bay and all its docks and boats. She ended up on the highway and saw a sign for the local college and decided to go take a look.

She was enjoying her walk and it felt so good to work her muscles. But it also dawned on her that she may have overdone on her allotted time since the university was quite the walk so she called Cain to let him know where she was.

"Thank you for the call, baby. I'm coming up to get you so stay put."

When Cain arrived, he wasn't mad and Becca's enthusiasm as always made him smile.

Once in the car he told she'd been gone over three hours and perhaps he should buy her a watch.

She told him she was sorry but it felt so great to stretch her legs. He just nodded.

Then she floored him and he nearly drove off the road.

"Cain, would you please fuck me tonight? I'm missing my favorite sex toy."

He pulled the car over to look at her. "Becca, you have impeccable timing. And I hate it when you use that word… but yes we can absolutely have sex." He shook his head.

She was grinning all the way back to the harbor.

This day was turning out to be quite lovely.

Becca's mood was jubilant and Joel took notice since she'd been a tad cold to him since he was one of the wardens of food intake.

She asked him, "What's for dinner?"

He asked if she was hungry and got a resounding 'no' but was still curious.

His response of salmon got a single nod… she wasn't a fan.

They had like one hundred and eighty pounds of halibut and she could eat that every night but they'd only had it twice since they'd been in Alaska.

She headed to their room but remembered her iPad was in his office so she turned to go grab it. Cain was right behind her. She jumped and he was grinning as he closed and locked the door. He had her in his arms taking full command of her lips. Their clothes were off in record time as well and he spent the afternoon helping her get her appetite back. And fulfilling his promise.

"So, baby, what would you like to do tomorrow?" He was caressing her back as she played with his chest hair.

"You're going to think it's crazy but I would like to go buy a pair of shoes. I found a place downtown before all hell broke loose with my health. It's called 'Shoefly'." She was smiling into his chest.

He asked if he got to take her and she nodded.

"Think you might like to read to me tonight? I've been missing that too." He had moved down to her caressing her ass and she lost her train of thought.

She moaned his name and they both forgot about his question.

Damn she had missed him.

Joel called them to dinner and she didn't want to eat. She wanted to stay in bed with Cain.

He got up and put on his jeans and shirt and held out a robe for her to put on.

"So, why do you get clothes and I only get a robe?" she asked as she was putting it on.

He wrapped his arms around her. "Because I like easy access." He patted her ass and took her hand as they headed to the dining room.

Joel put Cain's salmon dinner down first which he never did… it's always ladies first and that got an odd look from his employer but he winked and put down

Becca's meal next. It was a mushroom and cheese omelet with fresh tomatoes. She thanked him.

Cain also made him feel good about going the extra mile. "You're a good man, Joel, thank you."

With dinner complete, Cain asked again about reading that evening.

She finally had to tell him. "I sort of gave the book to Joel. He loved it by the way."

He kissed her hand and thanked her. "I didn't realize how wordy that book was going to be and we only made it through one chapter."

She laughed.

"So tonight, you can start 'Fifty Shades'." He was smiling and she no longer was laughing.

Her suggestion of 'Great Expectations' got a firm head shake.

CRAP!

"I will make you a deal. You only have to read the first two as your punishment but they will be read back to back." His stern look was still incredibly sexy.

She asked if she could start where he stopped and he told her from the beginning was fine.

'WELL HELL.'

She managed three chapters nestled in his arms before they both fell fast asleep.

GLACIER GARDENS

She was alone in bed, which she hated but it was the first time in over a week and he left a note.

'Early morning calls so I can play all day with you.' Forever 'C'.

She grabbed the note and kissed it. She really loved him. Once in her closet she put it with all the other notes she had kept and headed in for a shower.

Joel handed her a coffee and asked what she'd like for breakfast. She opted for poached eggs on toast. He smiled since usually she settled for whatever he put in front of her.

Cain came out as she was starting to eat and gave her a good morning kiss.

"I have a surprise for you today, after shoe shopping."

Joel couldn't help himself. "Shoe shopping, really?"

Becca felt like teasing him right back and cocked her head to the right and squinted and told him, "Careful Joel, your gay is showing."

Cain managed not to spray coffee all over himself and her that time but just. His expression however gave her the giggles again and Joel too.

Once composed.

"Miss Becca, I can't believe you said that." His look was supposed to be appalled but he missed it by a mile.

"Oh please. Ask Cain… I quite enjoy entertaining myself at others expense, frequently actually." She said it so deadpan followed by a bite of her eggs. Cain lost it. She'd never heard him get the giggles like that… he got up and walked away. Joel's expression was precious.

Now she wondered what her surprise was.

After breakfast she went and found him in their room. He had both their jackets. But they ended up on the floor as Cain tossed her on the bed, tickling her until she peed her pants.

He smiled. "Now we're even."

'ASS.'

She took a quick shower and changed. He was still smiling when she came out in fresh jeans and sweater. She took his hand and they headed through the salon and down to the docks for their outing.

"What's my surprise?"

He gave her a rather nice kiss and told her she'd have to wait until after she had new shoes.

They took the BMW and on the drive into town she plotted a bit of revenge for the tickling, but it would take scissors or a sharpie and some privacy.

"What are you overthinking now, Becca?" He caught her off guard and she jumped.

"Speculating about my surprise." Little white lie couldn't hurt and he just made her wet herself.

243

He took her hand, kissed it and held it the rest of the trip.

Juneau has a weird road system in the downtown area; too many one-way streets but they still managed to find the store and parking.

Thank God he was driving; parallel parking wasn't her strong suit.

Her best friend always told her it was because women's breasts get in the way. That always made her smile.

Once in the store it became clear that she was looking for comfort and he was looking for sexy.

He handed her a pair of CFM shoes with the highest heels she'd ever seen. "Really, CFM shoes," and shook her head.

She tried them on to make him happy but couldn't get her balance let alone walk in the damn things. He shook his head looking a bit disappointed.

He finally approved a pair of black ankle boots with a kitten heel and a pair of sandals that laced up her calf.

She looked at the price and put them both back. Thinking maybe tennis shoes at Fred Meyer.

"This was your idea remember and you said I could come so behave." He then told the salesgirl that they'd take both and handed her his credit card.

Becca noticed the looks of envy from half the women in the store and took hold of his hand with a tender squeeze. He gave her a 'you're welcome' kiss and winked at the salesgirl who blushed.

With packages in hand they headed back to the car. On the way Cain asked, "What does CFM stand for?"

"Come Fuck Me." His shocked expression might have been on her flat delivery in answering his query.

He put the packages in the backseat and opened her door, leaning down so only she could hear. "Baby, I don't need shoes for that." And patted her ass as she got in the car.

OH Yeah... HUGE blush.

They headed back towards the valley and made the turn at Fred Meyer. She couldn't think what they needed there but he didn't turn in, instead went around the corner and turned into 'Glacier Gardens Rainforest Adventure'. Her surprise.

She had read about it when she was under house arrest and was hoping they would have a chance to go there.

She was all smiles and gave him a very nice thank you kiss.

"Careful, baby, between the shoes and your kiss we may have to come back." She smacked his chest and started to take pictures of the fifteen-foot 'one of kind' flower towers.

Cain took her hand and led her down to the visitors' center to purchase their tickets.

Their guided tour was wonderful and Becca's zeal kept Cain enthralled as well.

They learned that this special botanical garden was fifty acres in size and was actually part of the Tongass

National Forest and therefore under its protection. There were flower towers throughout the garden created by 'Steve Bowhay', *he and his wife Cindy owned the facility.* When he was building the road system as the story goes, he got frustrated with a log that damaged a rented excavator. *'They only cut trees when absolutely necessary, they used mostly ones that had fallen by natural occurrences.'* Again, as the story goes, Steve grabbed a tree with his then injured excavator out of anger and slammed it into the ground several times leaving its roots up in the air, giving him the idea to plant fresh flowers and plants in the roots each and every year and the rest is history. They have each become their own work of art.

The scenic view point was spectacular. It sits about six hundred feet up Thunder Mountain and gave them a two hundred-degree view of Taku inlet, downtown Juneau, Douglas Island as well as the Mendenhall Valley and on the horizon, the Chilkat Mountain Range.

Lots of photos.

The tour ended way too soon for Becca's liking. But she got loads of pictures to remember every aspect of the garden.

She gave Cain a huge hug. "I love this surprise so much. Thank you for bringing me."

"You're most welcome, baby," and kissed her head. "How about some lunch?" She nodded into his chest.

He drove them back to Fred Meyer. Her look was quizzical but he opened her door and she took his hand.

They ended up with a selection of deli meat, cheese, a fruit selection, crackers and drinks. He also bought a blanket, knife and some napkins.

"Let's go drive out the road for a picnic." He was wearing her beloved smile. She nodded in full agreement.

They shared an apple on the trip out to 'Point Bridget State Park' which sits on Berner's Bay. And if you're curious… the road does end.

On the drive Becca spotted two deer and four porcupines.

Cain also pointed out Shelter and Lincoln Islands to her. She already knew the biggest one was Admiralty.

They walked around looking for a nice spot for lunch. Several people were camping and they didn't want to invade their space.

The other thing that enjoyed that park… mosquitoes.

After her third bite, Becca had had enough of nature. Cain agreed and they headed back to the car.

An hour later with the blanket spread out and all the food nicely displayed, both Cain and Becca enjoyed their picnic on the back deck of 'SIRA'.

It was the perfect end to their play day.

That night she read another two chapters which is where Cain had stopped his previous reading.

He told her that the next night would be all new to him.

She had other plans for the book. 'Paybacks my love.'

BEST LAID PLANS

She was wrapped in his arms when they awoke the next morning. Best way to start any day.

"Morning, baby."

"Hello, my love. What are your plans today?"

"I would like to stay in bed all day with you calling me 'my love' but I have a couple conference calls that need to be done this morning." He made a sad face.

She kissed him and started to get up… he pulled her back for a few more intimate kisses before finally letting her go.

They ate breakfast together before duty called Cain into his office and Becca needed to find scissors. A little redaction on their reading material was in order.

It took her the better part of an hour to get some of the steamier scenes removed and cut up into confetti.

She was in her closet with the door locked so no one would catch her and she noticed her second dress still hanging there. She'd never worn it.

And he did say he only needed to work in the morning.

A wicked idea formed in her head.

She went and brushed her teeth, put on extra perfume and the dress minus bra and panties.

She even put on the new sandals that laced up her calf. Not bad actually.

A little self-conscious about the cleavage but thought he'd enjoy that.

'Now, how to spring this on Cain.'

She didn't have to; he walked into the stateroom calling for her. "Baby, are you in here? I think today's schedule is getting changed."

She walked out of her closet and his eyes got wide and his smile got huge.

"DAMN, you look good. And smell divine. I wish I didn't have to leave."

She walked back into her closet and grabbed her robe covering up the outfit she had on.

He went and pulled her into his arms. "I'll be a few hours at a local investment group's office, so if you would be so kind as to wait for my return, I would like to take full advantage of you in that dress."

He left her with a very nice kiss and a smack on the ass that made her heart skip a beat or two.

She gave it a minute or two before she decided she needed to burn off her excess energy.

She threw the dress to the back of the closet and pulled on shorts, bra and workout top and headed for the gym.

Joel handed her a water as she walked by but didn't say a word.

Smart man.

She worked up a great sweat on the treadmill getting the level up to a nice healthy climb. She then worked with the dumb-bells... still trying to get her shoulder back into shape. Twenty reps on each arm and twenty more for good measure.

Now she needed another shower.

She missed her lake. She would love a swim right about now.

Joel gave her a protein shake as she walked by and she finished it before heading into the shower.

She wasn't about to go back into the hospital.

Freshly washed and no longer feeling sexy she put on sweatpants and an oversized T-shirt.

She handed Joel back the glass with a thank you and headed to the entertainment room.

With her own hunk busy she decided to watch 'The Avengers': lots of hunks to look at in that movie.

She'd still rather have hers.

The movie was just ending when Joel popped his head in and asked if she wanted lunch in there... she did and went ahead and put in the second 'Avengers' movie.

Keep the theme going.

He brought her a Caesar salad with blackened halibut and a bottle of water. She thanked him.

He knew her so well.

When the second movie was over and not wanting to watch another, she headed back down to return her lunch tray and to brush her teeth.

She met Cain on the stairs.

"Hi there, I'm sorry, it took a lot longer than I was expecting." Looking at her new outfit, "I'm sorrier you changed."

Her smile didn't reach her eyes as she kissed his cheek and told him she needed to brush her teeth.

Being ever the gentleman, he took the tray in one hand and hers in the other and walked her back into the salon.

He handed the tray to Joel as he escorted her to their room.

She headed into the bathroom.

When she came out, he had her dress in his hand. "Let's see about getting you changed, shall we?"

She moved away shaking her head.

"That shipped sailed, Mr Curtis," sounding quite resolved.

"Why, Ms Jackson, is that a challenge?" And he moved forward not giving her much room to maneuver.

She tried to run across the bed and got tackled halfway over.

"As I was saying, I want you back in the dress… now please," and he was helping remove her sweat pants.

She knew he wasn't going to give up and with a, 'you've kept me waiting all fucking day' look… she very curtly said, "Fine" and pulled off her shirt and pulled on the dress.

Her, "There… happy?" was a bit snippy too.

He shook his head with a huge smirk.

251

He loved her challenging him.

He then got up to help her remove the bra and panties she had left on. "We won't be needing these the rest of the night."

His kisses changed her mood pretty quick.

And they finally christened the last guest bedroom. Twice.

She even read him two more chapters and he didn't seem to notice that all the sex scenes had been omitted.

They had just had their own for the better part of the evening and he didn't need any ideas.

Later that night the weather changed and it started to pour.

Cain's mood changed a bit too.

JUNEAU–STILL

The weather was still horrible. As mentioned before, Juneau was a temperate rainforest and proving it the past several days.

Apparently, a huge typhoon in the Pacific Ocean was causing high winds in the Gulf and in turn causing all the rain throughout the region.

Six days of nonstop rain can be depressing for anyone.

Cain and the captain were now discussing heading south and trying another time to see the interior of Alaska.

Everyone was disappointed but none more than Cain.

He had planned this trip for well over a year.

Her upbeat and usually positive hunk was showing a chink in his armor for the very first time.

He was also having some work issues that he refused to talk about.

So, between work and the weather, Cain's mood had become surly.

Fact was his short temper was causing everyone to give him a wide berth and Becca started having serious doubts. She had had enough negativity for one lifetime, thank you very much.

She even avoided him on more than one occasion.

With him spending so many hours working, she occupied her days by taking a dozen or so walks, yes, in the rain. She also got the BMW keys and went to visit what Juneau calls a mall; they had two actually, and wandered around both. At least it was dry to walk in the malls. And she did find a great store called 'NAO' which stood for 'Nugget Alaskan Outfitters' and bought herself new tennis shoes. She worked out in the gym and actually got her shoulder feeling almost normal. And she read a lot, mostly in the first guest room since it was quiet.

She did whatever it took to keep busy and not disturb Cain.

It was rain day number seven and she woke up alone again that morning. It had been that way since the rains started. Well the day after, but still… too long. She missed him.

He was always there at night, but wasn't. She would still read to him and they cuddled but Becca could tell his mind was always somewhere far away. Even when he kissed her goodnight, there wasn't much feeling… he seemed empty of emotion.

They hadn't had sex since the dress day.

And 'NO' she wasn't going to put on another… this was different.

She never saw him at breakfast and sometimes he'd join her for lunch. But again... he wasn't really there and their conversations were always about the weather or quite generic for lack of a better word.

Too much time alone... the mind tends to overthink.

'Well, Becs, you knew it couldn't last forever'... happiness is fleeting so maybe their affair was coming to an end.

She never really told him where all her doubts came from, not really. He knew the highlights and that was more than enough... the rest would remain her deep dark little secret.

She was married for over twenty years but for the last fourteen she ended up being the breadwinner and the caregiver but never a wife. He wasn't just unkind to her when they did have a physical relationship. He was critical and spiteful. But she took those stupid vows to heart. Better or worse. She just didn't get much of the better part. She would chastise herself. 'Suck it up and get on with the hand you're dealt.' She did love him at first but with some major soul searching and self-honesty, she wasn't in love with him. Truth be told the last five years she thought more about leaving him. His negative and hateful attitude made her find ways to be away from him more and more. Her world was crushing her and there was no one who could help. Then her parents died and again no one was there to realize that her heart was breaking. She couldn't believe that her life was so pathetic. This brought on even darker thoughts. Ones that made her truly believe she wasn't worthy of happiness. She felt that, 'if this is all there is, why the fuck do I need to even be here?' Wishing she wouldn't wake up on some days. Once or twice thinking of helping that wish come true. Her angst was always there overwhelming her. A very sad existence. One she bore alone. One she hid quite nicely from all who knew her. Brave face and all.

She had spent the better part of that day worrying about the demise of their relationship so her mood had soured, self-induced but she didn't care.

Again, too much time on her hands and her feeling sorry for herself. 'Becs, you really need to just leave. It's almost time to get back to work anyway.' She hated that thought.

'Leave him…she didn't want to leave him. She loved him, more than she'd ever loved anyone. Ever'

During lunch that day, he asked if she'd like to go out to dinner. She did and a plan was set.

She was hoping this would put them back on the right track. Maybe have a serious conversation and she could find out what was really going on with him.

Not so much… he was still being distant.

She still couldn't help but notice the looks people gave them when they were out and it made her very self-conscious of their vast differences. Over fifty years of thinking one thing isn't removed because of a five plus week fantasy affair.

He was always getting flirted with so this night and his aloof attitude caused her to actually point out two very attractive women vying for his attention and so much more suited to his nine-year younger age and of course his amazing good looks.

She seriously wondered how he didn't notice.

It started out as sort of a joke, trying to get some reaction out of him. She hated him being so distant.

Plus, she was feeling a bit mean-spirited with her own self-doubt, which he warned her about.

'Note to self... always listen to your inner voice when it's screaming 'NO'!'

Boy did that idea ever backfire... she'd seen him pissed off on a few occasions so she knew the look but this was so much more intense.

She told him she was kidding and apologized but he was still fuming when they returned to the yacht.

They no more got back to their stateroom when he grabbed her and put her over his knee.

He had threatened this several times but she never thought he'd really do it.

The first smack was an attention getter for sure.

She struggled to get out of his grasp but he wasn't having any of that.

'How humiliating,' she thought... plus it stung.

One hand was holding her down and with the other he grabbed her waistband and pulled down both her pants and panties in one fluent move.

The next palm smack was on her now bare ass and it really hurt.

She again tried to get away. That brought on even harder smacks.

With each one he told her, "This will be the last time you bring up the subject of how I can do better or doubt how I feel about you. Do you understand?"

"Yes, I'm sorry. Please stop," she pleaded.

Smack number five or six. "You were teasing me? This is going to be one hell of a reminder not to do that again."

"Cain, I won't bring it up again. Stop."

"I warned you and still you pushed me," he scolded.

Smack number ten brought the spanking to its conclusion.

He was flexing his hand when he sat her up on the bed.

She wanted to stand but didn't dare. It hurt to sit.

He looked at her and made no apologies for what she thought was a tad overreaction BUT she knew better than to say anything, ever.

Without warning he took her face in his hands and kissed away the few tears that had managed to escape.

The *Traitors.*

He followed those kisses with a deep passionate one that took all thoughts of her sore ass away and left her gasping for air.

What that man could do with his tongue should be illegal. 'Fuck!'

He finished removing her pants, followed by her shirt and bra... then shed his clothing before reclaiming her mouth. They spent the next hour having the most erotic sex she'd ever had. Pink ass be damned, this man knew exactly how to leave her feeling quite sated and very wanted.

She would never doubt that again... or say it out loud at least.

Baby steps.

That night their intimacy went to a whole new level when he finally confided to her about his tumultuous week.

One of his very first clients who retired just three years prior had passed away. It was a shock to everyone who knew him and it hit Cain hard since they were also good friends.

On top of that the rain and grey gloomy weather and not getting to go into the interior didn't help either and he was feeling 'grief'. She held him tight and just listened. When finished he didn't look relieved just unburdened. And she thanked him for telling her.

That night he was wrapped in her arms with his head on her chest and she rubbed his back until he was fast asleep.

She thought about her own grief and realized that she'd not felt that heart-crushing anguish in some time. She had Cain to thank for that.

She loved him more than he'd ever know. 'Twitchy' and all.

BOUND FOR SOUTHERN WATERS

Her butt was a tad sore but her mood was quite over the moon.

Sometime during the night, they switched places since his arms were tightly wrapped around her now.

She realized that's what she'd been missing the past week and her tears hit his arm.

He tightened them around her. "Baby, what's wrong?"

"Nothing, I'm just incredible happy. I've really missed your arms in the morning."

He tightened his embrace even more and kissed her hair. "Me too. And I'm sorry I've been distracted. And thank you for listening last night. And just so you know, there is no place I'd rather be than right here with you."

"How's your ass by the way?" She knew he was smirking without looking.

"Sore." She was trying to sound angry… swing and a miss.

"Good." And turned her face towards his to give her a proper good morning kiss.

He got up to get in the shower.

She spent that time thinking about him.

He was the only man that ever left her feeling utterly spent. Which he'd done more than once.

He was exceptionally good at seduction and his stamina still took her breath away.

He also seemed to take great satisfaction if and when she tried to fight the inevitable and relished in making her entire body come alive.

And right when she didn't think she could take anymore... he found a way to get her body to rise to the occasion.

He loved to love her... he'd shown her that over and over the past several weeks.

Truth is, he wore her out on many a night. And on more than one occasion he spanked her, but it was for pleasure not a reprimand and she became very fond of his sexual prowess.

It wasn't all sex... he also knew how to make her smile and laugh.

Talk about a heady combination. He made her happier than she'd felt in a very long time. You might even say ever and she thanked God for letting Cain come into her life.

She was so deep in thought she didn't see him watching her until he spoke and she jumped. As usual.

"Baby, you are deep in thought. And that smile is very intriguing. Are you thinking about me?" She nodded and he gave her that smile that could melt every iceberg in Alaska.

He climbed back in bed. "I'm glad," and proceeded to give her another nice memory to think about while he was working.

This day was a thousand times better than the previous seven days and she could see everyone's mood changing.

The decision was made and they would be leaving for home that afternoon.

Joel was getting the shopping lists made and he and Frank would be taking the rental cars back after he was done.

The trip south would be six days to Seattle with two stops for fuel.

They would be hitting the worst of the rough water between Icy Strait and Sitka but the rest of the trip shouldn't be too bad.

Becca told Joel to pick up extra ginger and peppermint extract, just to be safe. He agreed.

The tides would be their highest just after five so that was their timetable and everyone was busy.

There wasn't much she could do... it sucks not having a job to help get ready for their departure.

During lunch, which she made since Joel was out shopping, she was wishing she could do more and her look must have been a bit brooding since he reminded her of her already sore ass.

She told him to put his itchy, bitchy, twitchy palm away. She just wished she could do more to help.

"Oh, okay. Well, help Joel when he comes back." She smiled and nodded.

But he couldn't help but inform her that the next time she doubted their bond he wouldn't stop until he was sure she couldn't sit for a month.

And with that rather 'in your face' threat, he gave her a very nice thank you for lunch kiss before heading back into his study.

Damn that man. Even his threat left her a bit breathless.

She really did need to make a better effort to curb the self-doubt. At least for the sake of her cute little behind since it took the brunt of her stupid mouth.

Cain for the most part was the most upbeat person she'd ever met.

And truth be told… she was in awe of him for that.

She needed to try harder to keep that glass half full.

It can be exhausting by the way.

But he was a marvelous influence.

Per Cain's suggestion, she did help Joel put all the new purchases away and helped him get everything latched down for their trip south.

A few hours later they were fueled and starting towards Chatham Strait. Homeward bound.

Cain found her reading in her favorite corner chair. She made room so he could sit next to her and he wrapped his arms around her and she laid her head on his chest. She loved him so much and wondered what he'd say if she told him.

"Baby, I need a nap and would like you to join me please." She nodded into his chest.

Joel woke them when dinner was ready.

It was cold by the time they came out.

He left them reheating instructions and both Cain and Becca had to laugh.

Poor Joel had done that several times throughout the course of their trip.

Cain loved to throw her off her game. "So tonight you get to start book two if memory serves."

CRAP!

She hadn't edited that book yet. But it wasn't that bad in the beginning; she might have time to take the scissors to it later.

She smiled when she remembered tossing the first book in the trilogy somewhere in Canadian waters weeks ago. That memory made her wish she could throw the second book into Alaskan waters.

"And, baby, please don't mutilate another book. I let you get away with it once but not again."

Well shit!

She just shook her head. She should have known. He is after all, very perceptive.

She started the second book that night… no editing allowed.

Becca liked that they were spending more time together on the trip south.

He still had to work in the mornings but she got most of his afternoons and all his nights.

DAY FOUR AT SEA — The Fight!

Reality bites.

The time finally came when the math she'd done in her head had to come out of her mouth.

Becca had taken a one-year sabbatical and she only had a couple of weeks left before she needed to return to the working class. This, for some odd reason, caused their biggest fight.

She mentioned she would have to head home from Seattle, which was less than thirty-six hours away, and she'd hope to see him after he was back in San Diego, the yacht's semi-permanent home.

"And you're just bringing this up now? Why the hell didn't you tell me you needed money?" He was miffed.

She couldn't understand the overreaction on his part. He knew she didn't have tons of money. Hell, he set up her autopay. And she'd never asked him for money. Why would she?

"Well, as I'm sure you know autopay is all well and good but one needs money in the bank to actually cover the bills. Money I can make with a job. Weird thought I know but that's the way it works."

"You know that sarcasm is the lowest form of humor. "He was frowning at her.

She informed him to suck it up.

"Becca, I swear to God, I'll put you back over my knee. I'm being serious here."

'Twitchy little fucker.'

She knew he was mad but she thought he looked sexy and that wasn't the best way to think at the time so she reminded him that 'the heart grows fonder'. He walked away.

Yep, lead balloon on the cutesy angle.

She didn't follow and thought letting him cool down at this point was a brilliant idea.

When he returned, he told her the kid would drive her car to San Diego and once moored he would drive her to her place in Nevada.

'How is that a solution?' she thought. That's just him getting his way.

'Fuck that,' she thought.

They both had a stubborn streak a mile wide… this impasse was the first major hurdle they needed to address. They had several minor ones along the way. In comparison.

At this point you should know the entire crew was more than likely hiding in the engine room with Frank.

He broke their silence when he asked her for access to her bank account again. He wanted to see where she was financially and to help figure out just how crucial it was that she get back to work before the trip was finished.

They had another week at least before reaching southern California. And he wanted her to stay on board.

He even went so far as to tell her at her age she should have planned better for retirement and for her aging needs.

Stop while you're behind, man.

Nope!

He then offered to be her financial advisor at no charge. He also told her to get an extension on her furlough and he'd put money in her account to cover all her bills for the next month or two.

That may have sounded reasonable to some and even generous but her hackles were way up. And with his overbearing attitude she wasn't about to give in.

It also made her realize just how different in age and status they were. And he knew full well why she didn't have much of a retirement and bringing it up now was 'fucking rude'.

'Maybe he should get me a walker while he's putting me out to pasture, jackass.' She was beyond pissed.

She had managed to think snarky remarks instead of saying them.

But her inner voice must have been hiding because all of sudden she said them out loud.

And just an FYI, name calling brings on a very quick and harsh twitchy palm.

She was heading to the bedroom when she was over his knee for a second time with five very powerful smacks.

If you're curious, 'Could you be a bigger Mother Fucking Condescending Jackass? Shove your money and advice up your ass,' did the trick.

Maybe over the top but she was angry and thought his reaction was way out of line as well.

She managed to apologize for the remarks because it was a low blow. But when he didn't express any regret for putting her over his knee again… she packed.

She and her bags were making their way to the guest room one floor up when she told him, "I realize we really do need a break so I'll move into your guest room for the duration of the trip and get off your yacht the minute we stop in Seattle. When you get back to California… I'll be at my home in Nevada if you decide you ever want to see me again."

Now she had to hurry and leave the main salon area before she cried in front of him, again. This time would be out of anger. She hated that she couldn't control her tear ducts when she was beyond mad. That weakness sucks. But she also knew they were coming.

His hand took hers as she reached for the stairway door, not forcefully but in a 'please don't do this' that made her breath catch and look at his pleading eyes.

Why…? For what reason would he need to have her never leave him for such a brief amount of time?

She went sightseeing without him, took walks and hikes without him and even went out shopping alone and never a word of disapproval or of his wanting to go with her. Mostly because he was working… but still. She was used to some independence.

She had to admit that she loved… really loved having him so attentive when they were together. 'Focus, Becs.'

Truth be told, it actually scared her a bit too, since she knew this depth of happiness she felt couldn't last forever.

'Could it?'

So, again she wondered, why was he making such a major issue with her going home?

It could be for less than two weeks when he could join her and after today, her sore ass could use the break from Mr Spanks and his overzealous twitchy palm.

'Becs, deal with the current situation,' she scolded herself.

She let him lead her to the couch in the living room and there they sat staring at each other. Her look of confusion and his of distress.

She finally broke the silence. "Please explain yourself, because so far it's been a bit unclear as to why my leaving and going back to work is an issue. You work all the time."

He sighed and looked into her eyes with a blazing look that she'd not seen often. "Becca, baby, do you believe home is where your heart is?" She nodded because she really did.

"But you keep saying you're going home. And since you believe home is where your heart is... you are home, with me, here... now and forever. "He took her right hand and removed the lovebird ring and placed in on her left hand kissing it.

That statement and gesture caught her off guard and left her completely silent.

He, of course, was right, but neither of them had really said the three little words except maybe during sex and that didn't count in her mind but maybe it did in his.

This declaration on his part... was overwhelming and the tears that threatened during her anger came before she even realized just how emotional she felt about what he said and did.

He had her in a vise-gripping hug, kissing her hair, cheeks, lips and wiping away the tears as he went, even before she had a chance to blink.

So, there it was... he made his intentions known just five and a half weeks after they'd met. She felt like the universe picked the wrong woman... she'd never been lucky in love, ever.

But she loved this man with every bit of her heart and soul and had been so very afraid to say it aloud and now it was out there and she couldn't speak with the huge lump in her throat.

His arms never released her and she felt safe and incredibly cherished.

Once her heart and breathing cooperated she managed a weak, "You're right, you own my heart and have for some time now. And home is wherever you are."

She could feel his smile and settled into his warm embrace.

His lips by her ear, "I love you, Rebecca Lynne Jackson and I never want to live a minute without you."

She knew she wasn't going anywhere without this man. Her man. The man she loved beyond reason.

He won the battle, the war and her heart with one simple statement.

Damn, he doesn't play fair. Thank God!

A SUNNY TUESDAY

She woke with a start and felt very stiff. With a yawn
and a stretch, she realized that both her back and neck
were way out of sorts.

*Note to self, 'Never fall asleep in an Adirondack
chair.'*

*Second note to self, 'Don't stay up so late watching
a movie you've seen a hundred fucking times before.'*

*But what woman doesn't love 'Steel Magnolias'? It
was one of Mary's all-time favorite movies. 'A Good
memory to be sure.'*

She had a rather lovely and somewhat erotic dream.
And that made her blush. She hated that the details
faded so quickly when it came to daydreams. It left her
happy and a bit sad at the same time. 'How odd,' she
thought.

The lake, her lake was lovely this morning.

She always enjoyed her stay at the family cabin.
She missed her mom and dad. They had both passed
away almost four years ago now, but her brother was
coming out in a week for a short stay and she was
looking forward to spending time with him.

*She'd have to remember to get groceries before he
arrived. He always bitched when he thought she wasn't*

eating. 'Big Brother prerogative' is what he'd always tell her. 'Jackass'.

She was watching an osprey flying low and looking for a bit of breakfast; sushi, she thought and laughed out loud.

She truly loved this lake and was looking forward to a swim later when the day warmed up a bit. She was no longer able to stay in the chilly water for hours like she did as kid.

Still, the lake brought her peace.

Just a couple weeks more weeks and she'd be heading back to her real life.

Don't misunderstand, she loved Alaska and her life in Sitka, which was part of the Inside Passage, and a rainforest, which some people don't know.

She also loved being able to teach the next group of marketing executives but she relished her summer break back in the lower forty-eight. Spending time on her lake. It really was the best of both worlds.

Usually when she was down, she'd spend a couple of weeks in Nevada with her best friend.

But cancer took her eight months ago and that still brought tears to her eyes.

Mary was her best friend for over twenty-five years. And was the one who convinced her to get a divorce the year prior and find the happiness she deserved. Find love.

She was still working on the last part, a promise she made to Mary. Damn, she missed her friend. It always made her heart hurt... she wondered if she'd ever feel whole again.

The tears came. 'Damn it.'

Her sip of coffee was less than pleasant, it was cold.

"Well, that's disgusting," and then wondered to herself,

'Wow, how long was I asleep?'

She rose to go refresh her cup and get a tissue when she heard that annoying sound.

Jet ski... the quiet breakers on the lake. She wasn't a fan.

Not her concern right now; coffee was her only agenda. Well that and a Kleenex.

Suddenly the sound ended and that did catch her by surprise. Jet skis don't just stop unless a rider has been thrown off.

She turned to see if everything was all right since it sounded close.

There he was at the end of her dock. A very handsome man was smiling at her.

The sun was making his green eyes sparkle. "Would a lovely lady spare a cup of coffee, bit cool on the water this morning?"

'Nice smile,' she thought. And nodded.

Something about this seemed so familiar.

Definitely a déjà vu moment.

'Focus, Becs'... Right, coffee... "How do you take it?"

He was walking towards her and pulled her into a very unsuspecting hug. And it felt nice.

Actually, it felt scarily familiar…

When his strong arms released her, he said, "Sorry, you just looked like you needed a friendly hug. "And wiped away a tear on her cheek.

He really did have quite a nice smile and was way handsome.

She thanked him for being so incredibly thoughtful.

She pointed to her coffee cup.

"I take a little milk in my coffee, thanks. I'm Curtis, by the way, Curtis Kane."

She gasped …

CPSIA information can be obtained
at www.ICGtesting.com
Printed in the USA
FSHW010127200320
68200FS